BIGGLES & CO.

'Now listen, Bigglesworth; I'll tell you what I'm prepared to do, and you can please yourself what you do about it. Run this gang of crooks to earth, or point out to me the man who is at the head of it—or the chief operator in this country—and I'll make you a present of a cheque for ten thousand pounds. That is a personal matter between ourselves. To that sum my firm will add another five thousand.'

Biggles drew a deep breath. 'That's a lot of money,' he said quietly.

'It is, but if it ever finds its way into your pocket you will have earned it, if I know what I'm talking about,' returned Brunswick grimly.

BIGGLES & CO.

CAPTAIN W. E. JOHNS

RED FOX

Red Fox would like to express their grateful thanks for help
given in preparing these new editions to Jennifer Schofield,
author of *By Jove, Biggles*, Linda Shaughnessy of A. P. Watt Ltd
and especially to John Trendler, editor of *Biggles & Co*, the
quarterly magazine for Biggles enthusiasts.

A Red Fox Book
Published by Random Century Children's Books
20 Vauxhall Bridge Road, London SW1V 2SA

A Division of the Random Century Group
London Melbourne Sydney Auckland
Johannesburg and agencies throughout the world

First published by Oxford University Press 1936

Red Fox edition 1992

Set in 10.5/12pt Baskerville
Phototypeset by Intype, London
Made and printed by Cox & Wyman Limited, Reading, Berkshire

ISBN 0 09 993800 6

Contents

The word 'Hun' used in this book was the generic term for anything belonging to the German enemy. It was used in a familiar sense, rather than derogatory. Witness the fact that in the R.F.C a hun was also a pupil at a flying training school.

W.E.J

Chapter 1

The Proposition

I

Major James Bigglesworth, D.S.O., D.F.C., more often known as 'Biggles', glanced down over the side of the aeroplane he was testing to where his two friends, Algy Lacey, of his old squadron, and 'Ginger' Hebblethwaite, his youthful protégé, were waiting impatiently outside the hangars ot Brooklands Aerodrome. With the familiarity of long practice he throttled back the engine, eased the joystick forward, and then side-slipped steeply towards the ground, levelling out over the famous motor track to glide in to a clean, three-point landing. The machine finished its run within a dozen yards from where the others were standing.

'There's a fellow waiting to speak to you,' Algy told him, as he jumped to the ground, pushed up his goggles, and began unbuttoning his leather coat.

'What does he want?'

'He won't say.'

'Who is he?'

'I've no idea. I told him I was a friend of yours, but he just said he'd wait. Seems a churlish sort of cove — this is him, coming now.'

Biggles stepped forward and looked up inquiringly as a dark, broad-shouldered, heavily built man of about fifty years of age approached confidently. He was immaculate in town clothes of perfect cut, wore a bowler hat, and carried an umbrella over the crook of his arm; altogether an unusual figure to be seen in an aerodrome normally devoted to sporting flying.

'Major Bigglesworth?' he inquired, in a brisk, almost peremptory tone, as he walked up.

'That is my name, sir,' replied Biggles evenly. 'Can I do something for you?'

'I would like to have a few words with you,' replied the other.

'Well, here I am. There's nothing to stop you,' smiled Biggles.

'I'm sorry, but—' The stranger indicated the others who were standing near, with a slight inclination of his head.

'They needn't stop you,' Biggles assured him quietly. 'They're both old friends of mine.'

'My business is of a very confidential—I might say secret—nature.'

'I've no secrets from my friends,' Biggles told him frankly.

'I'd rather speak to you alone. By the way, Colonel Raymond suggested that I came.'

Biggles started. 'Raymond, eh?' he ejaculated. 'Why didn't you say that at once? But what's the hurry? Couldn't you have 'phoned me, and asked me to meet you in town?'

'The matter is pressing. I've just spoken to Colonel Raymond at Scotland Yard. He looked you up in the telephone directory and rang up your rooms, but was told you were here. So I came down immediately in my car.'

Biggles looked past the speaker's shoulder to where a Rolls-Royce, with a liveried chauffeur in the driver's seat, stood outside the club-house. 'What's Raymond doing at Scotland Yard?' he asked with interest. 'He was my Wing Intelligence Officer during the war; we had some great times together.'

'So I gather. He is now Assistant Commissioner of Police. Didn't you know?'

Biggles opened his eyes wide. 'No,' he confessed, 'I'm dashed if I did. I'm glad to hear it, anyway, for he is a great scout.'

'Well, he advised me to see you.'

'Then it must be something important.'

'It is — very important.'

'I see. Very well, then.' Biggles turned to the others. 'Hang around for a bit; I'll be back presently,' he told them, and then led the way to the club-house 'Now, sir,' he continued, when they had found a quiet corner, 'what's the trouble?'

The stranger took a card from a case and passed it across the table.

Biggles took it and looked at it curiously. This is what he saw:

PAUL CRONFELT

Bullion Brokers.   *Cronfelt & Carstairs*
Dealers in Precious Stones.   *Lombard Street, E.C.*

He handed it back with a faint smile. 'If it's bullion or diamonds you want, I'm afraid there's nothing doing,' he murmured. 'I've never had any quantity of either.'

'I've quite a lot of both,' replied the other coolly, 'and that is why I'm here. I want to start an airline.'

Biggles raised his eyebrows. 'Well, that shouldn't be difficult. What's stopping you?' he inquired.

Cronfelt ignored the question. 'Could you run an airline?' he asked abruptly.

'I've never tried, but I shouldn't be surprised if I could,' returned Biggles.

The other settled himself a little lower in his chair and leaned forward confidentially. 'I can see you do not take the matter very seriously,' he said quietly. 'Perhaps I had better explain the position more clearly.'

'That would be a good idea. I'm listening,' Biggles told him.

Cronfelt took out a cigar, lighted it, and glanced round, presumably to make sure that no one was within hearing. 'We—that is, my firm, Cronfelt and Carstairs—are, as my card informed you, dealers in gold and precious stones,' he began. 'Now, as you must be aware, the instability of currencies in Europe and America at the present time makes it necessary for shipments of gold to be made from one country to another. When that happens, speed is everything, for two very good reasons. In the first place the gold is earning no interest while it is in transit; and in the second, there is always the risk of a currency fluctuation which may seriously affect the deal. That is why gold is now nearly always sent by air.'

'Yes, I understand that.'

'Very well. Now then. Up to the present, or to be more accurate, until recently, it has been the practice of my firm to send metal abroad, when the necessity arose, by an established air operating company. Usually it went from Croydon. You have no doubt seen references made in the newspapers to shipments of gold by air; I suppose they think the idea is still novel, but actually it has been going on for years.

'Now we had no trouble of any sort until about eight months ago, when we sent a large consignment of gold— nearly forty thousand pounds' worth—to Paris. It went in a large airliner. By a piece of good fortune, there happened to be a full quota of passengers that day on the regular service, which made it impossible to send the gold in the same aeroplane; so at the last minute a special one was put on. It crashed in northern France. Both pilots and the wireless operator were killed. You may remember the occurrence.'

'Was that the crash in which Geoffrey Lyle was killed?'

Cronfelt nodded. 'That was it,' he said.

Biggles puckered his forehead. 'But I didn't see anything about gold in the papers, and I read the case carefully,' he exclaimed. 'I knew Lyle well.'

'No, you didn't, for the simple reason that the papers knew nothing about the gold—at least, not at the time. The police suspected foul play and issued only half a story to the press. We, the airline authorities, the insurance brokers, and the police alone knew about the gold.'

'But why should the police suspect foul play?'

Cronfelt studied the glowing end of his cigar for a moment. Then he looked up. 'Because,' he said slowly, 'the gold disappeared.'

'Good heavens!'

'What is more, it has never been recovered,' added Cronfelt.

A low whistle escaped Biggles' lips. 'That puts a different complexion on the crash,' he admitted.

Cronfelt smiled wanly. 'I thought you'd think that,'

he said. 'But let me go on: I haven't finished the story by a long way. The immediate result of that crash was an increase in the insurance rates. That may not convey much to you, but it meant a lot to us. In fact, it meant that unless there was a fairly wide margin of profit on the turnover, the insurance and freight charges absorbed it all. However, we went on, and several small consignments got through all right. Then we sent another big lot. It never arrived.'

'Stolen *en route*, eh?'

'We don't know. The machine never arrived.'

'What do you suppose happened to it?'

Cronfelt shrugged his shoulders. 'That's what we should like to know. Some pieces of wreckage—fabric and splinters—were found floating in the Channel, so it was assumed the machine was lost at sea. It was one of the twin-engined sort—I forget the name. There were four passengers on board, as well as the pilot. Their bodies were never found.'

'That's pretty grim.'

'Very grim indeed. Result, another increase in insurance rates, and, what is worse, a disinclination on the part of the airline people to touch the gold at all. A rumour about the metal leaked out, and passengers began to jib at travelling when there was gold on board.'

'I should think so, too.'

'Precisely. We ourselves could appreciate the point of view both of the public and of the airline people. Still, what was to be done? Well, the problem was solved for us in an unexpected way. A new German private company operating between European capitals approached us, and gave us a cut rate for transportation. The insurance rates were still high, of course, but the cut transport rate balanced them. We accepted, and as

12

before all went well while we were only shipping small loads. Then, about a month ago, we sent a parcel of very good diamonds to Amsterdam. They were taken by a special courier. The machine arrived, but—'

'The courier didn't?'

'Exactly. I see you keep up with a story very well.'

'What happened to him?'

'We've no idea. It was presumed that he fell out of the machine whilst it was over the sea. A body was subsequently washed up, and identified as that of our courier, but it had been ravaged by sea-water, and it may or may not have been him. The body was naked, so of course the diamonds were not recovered.'

'Nasty business.'

'Apparently that is what the insurance people thought. They settled our claim, but the sum was a big one, and they set inquiries afoot. As a result of those inquiries they have issued us with a notice to the effect that they will not cover any more of our gold or diamond shipments while we employ the German transport company.'

'But there must be other insurance companies?'

'There are, but the one we dealt with was the largest, and the course they adopt goes for all. The German people are very sore about it, naturally, because it reflects badly on their reputation.'

'But what about the other bullion dealers? Haven't they had any trouble?'

'Their experience has been very much the same as ours, but we have been the biggest sufferers. Only one or two other firms deal with metal on the same scale as ourselves. As with us, one company had a load of gold disappear *en route*, and on another occasion a consignment was stolen at the airport.'

13

'I see,' replied Biggles slowly. 'I'm beginning to get the drift. Your idea is to run your own line?'

'That's it. Naturally, we shall not be concerned with passengers. It will be a private venture, financed by ourselves with the primary object of carrying our own freight, but open to carry other people's as and when circumstances permit. It is probable that we shall get charters from other bullion dealers.'

'But that would hardly be an airline,' Biggles pointed out. 'As I see it, you propose to own one or two aeroplanes that will be open to charter, but the transport of your own stuff would be the first consideration.'

'That is really what it amounts to. I might say that we didn't think of it. Scotland Yard has been interested in the train of events, and the other day Carstairs, my partner, whom I hope you will meet some time, went to the Yard and asked for advice. To be quite candid, I knew nothing about it, but he came back full of the idea. Colonel Raymond was the man he saw, so I went along this morning and had a few words with him myself. He was all in favour of the arrangement, and recommended—strongly recommended—me to come to you.'

'And you want me to run the thing for you?'

'If you will.'

'Have you any idea of how much such a show would cost, or for that matter, how much an aeroplane costs?'

'None whatever.'

'At a rough guess, I should say it will take fifty thousand pounds to start this concern in a business-like way. Running expenses are high, apart from the initial cost of machines.'

Cronfelt smiled. 'I thought you were going to say half a million,' he said. 'Fifty thousand pounds is a small

14

sum compared with the value of the freights we handle. You needn't worry about the financial side, if that is all it amounts to. If we do go on with it, we shall, of course, do the thing properly. Well, what do you say?'

'Will you give me a few hours to think it over?'

'Certainly. The matter is urgent, but there is no immediate hurry for a day or two. I hope you will join us, Major Bigglesworth. Naturally, we need a man who is both competent and reliable, and Colonel Raymond assures me that you possess both these virtues in a high degree.'

'That's very kind of him,' replied Biggles. 'Look, Mr. Cronfelt, let us get this clear at the beginning. If I undertake this project I shall stipulate three things. They are definite, and as far as I am concerned, absolutely final.'

'And they are?'

'One: I shall need staff. I can't run a thing like this single-handed.'

'Naturally.'

'I should demand to engage my own staff. I need hardly say that they would be men whose integrity is beyond question, men whom I have known for years.'

'That's reasonable. Go on.'

'Two: I should have to be at liberty to choose my own equipment.'

'We should expect you to; we're not air experts.'

'Three: I should want to run the thing my own way, without interference from you or any one else. You hand the freight to me at the aerodrome, and I'll do my best to see that it reaches its destination, but how I do it is nobody's business.'

Cronfelt hesitated. 'That might be awkward,' he mused.

'It might, from your point of view, but it would be a thundering sight more awkward for me if my machine shed its wings in the air. On your own admission, and without mincing matters, there's dirty work afoot. That being so, I handle things my own way or not at all.'

'But my partner and I—'

'I'm not prepared even to discuss the matter, Mr. Cronfelt,' put in Biggles brusquely. 'As I see it, you stand to lose some money, but I stand to lose my life. I set some value on it, so I shall expect to be paid in proportion to the risk; but more important is the fact that I must run things exactly as I like, without consulting even you. A secret shared by two or three people is no longer a secret. If I know that only I know what I am doing, I shall know that no one else knows—which is a ham-fisted way of putting it, but you see what I mean?'

'Clearly, and I must confess that in your position I should feel the same way about it. Very well, I'm agreeable; it only remains for you to agree and my partner to consent for you to go straight ahead. We should allow you to get everything you would be likely to require, having the accounts sent direct to us for payment. I should place a small sum of money in the bank, say a thousand pounds, in your name, on which you could draw to meet petty cash outlay. That would save you running to us for every shilling.'

'That's generous of you,' acknowledged Biggles. 'Well, I'll think it over and let you have my answer to-night.'

'Shall I ring you up, or will you ring me?'

'You ring me, about ten o'clock, at my rooms. Here's my card—the 'phone number is on it. I take it you've no objection to my mentioning the matter to my two friends outside? They're pilots. They've flown with me through all sorts of weather, and if I join you they will come with me.'

'They will, of course, regard the matter as confidential?'

'What I tell them will go no farther, you may be quite sure of that,' Biggles assured him, as he stood up and saw Cronfelt to the door.

The bullion merchant took his seat in the Rolls. 'Ten o'clock,' he called, as the car glided away.

Biggles watched it disappear round the bend with a strange expression on his face. Then, deep in thought, he made his way back to the tarmac.

II

Later, in his rooms, he pushed back his coffee cup and glanced at the clock. 'Nine o'clock' he observed. 'We've got an hour to make up our minds.'

'Why *our* minds?' asked Algy quickly. 'You—'

'I've told you the story pretty well word for word as he gave it to me because I want you to know just where we stand, and I'm not going on with this show without you. I can't handle it single-handed, and I wouldn't if I could; I certainly wouldn't chip in with strangers. It would be folly on a job of this sort. Either we take it on or we don't. Which is it to be?'

'In other words, you're leaving the decision to me?'

'That's about it. If you say "No", then I'm through. Say "Yes", and we're both in it up to the ceiling.'

'I'm full out for it,' put in Ginger.

'No doubt; but you'll do as we do,' Biggles told him.

'Quite right, Chief,' answered Ginger quickly.

Algy rested his elbows on the table and ran his hands through his hair. 'I don't know what to say, and that's a fact,' he confessed. 'We've never tackled anything quite like this before. Why should we do it? What are we going to get out of it? Not very much, as far as I can see. We can't, in reason, ask for salaries that will make us rich for life, or anything like that; and it isn't as if we were in urgent need of money. Boiled down, it looks rather as if we should be taking on unknown risks without anything worth while to compensate for them. I don't mind a bit of trouble, but when it comes to taking on a bunch of crooks who are not beyond crashing a pilot for his cargo, just for the sake of obliging this fellow Cronfelt—well, it isn't my idea of a business proposition. I'm getting old, and maybe I'm getting nervous.'

Biggles nodded. 'That's just about how I feel,' he said quietly. 'Is it worth it? That's the question I have been asking myself all the afternoon. Frankly, I don't think it is. I can get all the kick I want out of flying without taking on a job as a ferry pilot*, for that is what it amounts to. If things went well we should soon get bored with it; if they went wrong we might land ourselves in a nasty mess. If it were left to me to decide, my answer would be "No". Which, between you and me and the gate-post, is why I have left the decision to you.'

'Well, I think the same as you,' returned Algy, 'so there seems to be no object in pursuing the debate. "No" it is, as far as I'm concerned. Cronfelt will have no difficulty in finding some one else to do it.'

'Good, that's settled then; let's—' Biggles broke off as a knock came on the door.

It was opened to admit Mrs. Symes, the housekeeper. 'There's a lady to see you, sir,' she said.

* During the First World War, pilots who flew aeroplanes to and fro across the Channel were known as 'ferry pilots'.

'A lady!' Biggles frowned. 'What sort of a lady?'

'Oh, quite a lady, sir.'

'But I don't know any ladies. She must have come to the wrong house.'

'Oh, no, sir, she asked for you personally.'

'What is her name?'

'She didn't give her name.'

'Oh, come on, Biggles, you can't keep a lady waiting,' protested Algy.

'No, I suppose not,' agreed Biggles awkwardly. 'All right, Mrs. Symes, ask her to come in. And don't stare at the door as if you'd never seen a lady before,' he added, turning to the others.

There was a curious silence as the door was pushed open and a remarkably pretty girl, who wore an expensive fur coat over her evening gown, walked in.

'Good evening, Major Bigglesworth,' she said without hesitation, looking directly at Biggles.

'How did you know which was me?' asked Biggles in surprise.

'I've had you pointed out to me; in fact, I've seen you several times,' replied the visitor.

'I'm afraid I can't return the compliment,' replied Biggles slowly.

The girl laughed. 'You're not very gallant, are you?' she protested. 'You have seen me, but you may not have noticed me.'

'Where?'

'At Heston and Hanworth. I think I saw you once at Brooklands. I do a little flying myself, you see.'

Biggles pulled out a chair. 'Is that what you've come to tell me?' he inquired.

The girl shook her head. 'No,' she said, suddenly

19

becoming serious. 'I rather wanted to talk to you—alone.'

'You're the second person who has said that to me to-day,' Biggles told her.

'I suppose Mr. Cronfelt was the other?'

There was a momentary silence. 'Cronfelt? Who's Cronfelt?' asked Biggles, a trifle harshly.

'My father's partner. My name is Carstairs, Stella Carstairs. I act as my father's private secretary. I was present when Mr. Cronfelt returned to the office this morning and discussed the result of his conversation with you at Brooklands.'

Biggles sat down suddenly. 'Well?' he said suspiciously.

'That's what I've come to see you about.'

'Then perhaps it will save you some time and trouble if I tell you right away that we have decided not to accept his proposal,' said Biggles quietly.

The girl caught her breath sharply. 'Oh, I *am* glad,' she cried.

Biggles frowned. 'Would it be impertinent to ask why?' he said curiously.

'No. I am glad because this thing is much deeper than you have been given to understand. Large sums of money are at stake between men who are utterly unscrupulous, men of a type that you may never have met, and would not understand if you did. They're—pagans. Twentieth-century infidels who worship the golden calf with such fervour that life, death, and suffering mean nothing to them.'

'Come, that's a bit steep, isn't it? Have you forgotten that your father is a bullion dealer?' murmured Biggles.

The girl's nostrils quivered. 'He is,' she admitted. 'But, please God, he won't be one much longer. He's lost most of his money, and I am hoping that he'll yield to my entreaties to withdraw from the concern before he loses everything we possess.'

'How about Cronfelt?'

'I know nothing about his financial affairs except that, unlike my father, he has more than one interest.'

'You don't like him, eh?'

'Why do you say that?'

'It just struck me that way, that's all.'

'Perhaps you're right, but it would be only fair to say that my prejudice—we'll call it that—is due to purely personal reasons.'

A hard look came into Biggles' eyes. 'Ah, I see,' he said softly. 'But there,' he went on quickly, 'we're not going on with the show, so there is really no point in discussing these things, Miss Carstairs, is there?'

'None at all. I'll be going. Kindly forget my visit and its object. My only excuse for coming is that I have been very worried lately, and I hated to see other people drawn into our affairs. I know about your war record, and I just couldn't let you walk into this trap, for that is what it is, without warning you—' She broke off as the telephone whirred shrilly.

Biggles picked up the receiver. 'Bigglesworth here,' he said.

'Hold the line, please,' came the voice of the operator. 'Long distance call for you. . . . Hello, Berlin . . . here you are.'

'Is that Major Bigglesworth?' said a quiet voice in perfect English.

'Bigglesworth speaking. Who are you?'

'Pardon my seeming discourtesy if I do not tell you,' replied the voice. 'Regard me as a friend, an admirer, who is sincerely anxious for your safety. I have rung up to say, do not in any circumstances accept the proposal that has been made to you to-day. Believe me, I speak with real sincerity. Keep out, and the incident, as far as we are concerned, is closed. Go on with it, and you may pay for your temerity with the life you have been so fortunate to keep for so long. Good-bye.'

Biggles' face hardened as he jangled the instrument. 'Hello . . . hello. . . .'

'The line's cleared,' came the voice of the operator.

Biggles put down the receiver and turned slowly to where the others were watching him. His face was set and a trifle pale.

'Who was it?' asked Algy sharply.

Biggles repeated the conversation as nearly as he could recall it, and then turned to where Stella Carstairs was still standing just inside the door. 'One thing is very clear,' he observed. 'The Intelligence Service of your father's enemies leaves nothing to be desired.'

'Seems to have shaken you,' ventured Algy.

'It has,' confessed Biggles. 'You see — I thought — '

'Well?'

'I thought I'd heard that voice before — a long, long time ago.' Biggles put his hand to his forehead. 'Where? . . . When?'

He swung round as the telephone again clamoured its summons. 'What a night we're having,' he muttered as he picked up the receiver. 'Hello . . . hello, yes,' he called, glancing at the clock. 'Bigglesworth speaking. Oh, it's you, Cronfelt . . . quite right; it's exactly ten o'clock. Yes, I've thought the matter over and reached a decision. My answer is — yes! Good-night.'

Chapter 2
The First Round

I

Exactly a fortnight later Biggles stepped out of the lift in the Lombard Street offices of Cronfelt & Carstairs, Ltd., and ignoring the general inquiry bureau, made his way briskly to a door on which was affixed a small framed notice bearing the single word 'Private'. He rapped lightly, and without waiting for the reply, entered. "Morning, Miss Carstairs,' he called cheerfully to the sole occupant of the room. 'Is the head lad about?'

'Mr. Cronfelt is with my father in his office,' she smiled. 'They're expecting you. Go right through—you know the way.'

Biggles walked across familiarly to the inner office, for during the past two weeks he had found it necessary to call several times to discuss contingencies that had arisen in connexion with the scheme. But at the door he paused. 'Feeling better about things now?' he asked quietly, glancing back over his shoulder.

Stella Carstairs sighed. 'Yes—and no,' she answered enigmatically. Suddenly she left her work and crossed the room swiftly. 'For the last time, don't do it,' she breathed earnestly, with her eyes on the door. 'Cry off; there is still time. My father won't mind, I know.'

'How do you know?'

'Because I have told him what I think about all this.

I've told him what I told you: that I am convinced that the project will arouse the antagonism of forces of which we know nothing, but will prove to be far-reaching in their influence. I can't tell you why, but I'm—afraid.'

'You mean, for your father?'

'And for you. I hate to see you being drawn into this war, for it is nothing less than that.'

'I know a little of war,' Biggles reminded her.

'You may, but not of this kind,' she replied swiftly. 'In the war that you know you could see your enemy. You always knew where to look for him; and when you found him it was legal for you to strike him down. This is different. The enemy may not be where you expect to find him. He may be behind you all the time. And when he strikes he will use weapons more deadly than those you know, because they are unseen and unsuspected.'

'Well, those I know can make an awful mess of a fellow,' smiled Biggles.

'You laugh, but it is no joking matter. Please withdraw from this crazy scheme—for my sake. You see,' continued Stella quickly, 'if you refuse to go on, my father will leave this firm. He is only staying now because you are associated with us. I think it was something Colonel Raymond told him about you that makes him so confident of your success. Be that as it may, there is no doubt that he takes an entirely different view of the whole thing now that he has met you and knows that you are handling our transport business.'

'Which is all the more reason why I can't let him down,' Biggles told her seriously. 'No, Miss Carstairs, what I start I finish. Your father has taken some hard knocks, financially. Never retire when you are getting hard knocks. The thing is to go on, and do a bit of hard knocking yourself—at least, that's my way.'

'And this is your last word?'

'It must be.'

'Then I have nothing more to say.'

Biggles watched her return to her desk, and then knocked on the door.

'Ah! There you are, Bigglesworth; dead on time,' greeted Cronfelt genially.

'An old military custom,' smiled Biggles. 'Good morning, Mr. Carstairs,' he added, turning to a frail, aristocratic old man who sat at the far end of the table.

'Good morning, Bigglesworth,' replied Carstairs. 'I hope you have come to tell us that you are all ready for action.'

Biggles threw his hat into the corner and pulled up a chair. 'Yes,' he said cheerfully, 'we're all ready. You asked particularly that the show should be ready to function to-day, so I take it there is a job of work on hand.'

'Quite right,' replied Carstairs tersely. 'The money market has worked out just as I expected it would, so we shall have to make a shipment of metal to Paris. You've got everything you require in the way of equipment?'

'Everything. There has been no difficulty in organizing on the lines I set out in my schedule. We're registered as a private company with a hangar of our own at Hardwick Airport. The machine we shall use for shipments is a Cormorant twin-engined biplane of the ordinary communication class. Normally, it is a six-seater, but as we shouldn't be likely to want all the seats I've cleared out four of them to make room for freight, although there is a compartment in the rear for luggage. It—'

'Never mind the details,' broke in Cronfelt. 'If you're satisfied, then we are. What about staff?'

'Four is the total, including myself. I've got Lacey and Hebblethwaite as extra pilots, although Hebblethwaite is a very good ground engineer as well. My old flight sergeant, Smyth, is the only other member. He's an expert fitter and rigger, and well able to do the ordinary maintenance service we shall require. In the case of anything serious the machine would, of course, go back to the makers. That's customary.'

'I see. Oh—I meant to have asked you. Under what name have you registered the company?'

Biggles smiled, took a slip of pasteboard from his pocket and tossed in on to the table.

Cronfelt picked it up, and as he read it a sudden frown puckered his forehead.

'What's this?' he said. 'Biggles & Co?'

'That's it. Anything wrong with it?'

'Er—no, I suppose not. It struck me that it sounded a little bit frivolous, though, that's all.'

'There are some people in the world who will not find it in the least frivolous,' replied Biggles slowly. 'We had to find a name, and for reasons of my own— call it conceit if you like—I wanted to be associated with it. But Bigglesworth is a bit long-winded. Moreover, people might wonder who it was. Those who really matter know me as Biggles.'

'I understand. And you are all ready to operate to-day?'

'Just as soon as I can get back to the aerodrome.'

'Splendid! Then you'd better get off and stand by. A big consignment of metal will reach you by road at twelve o'clock. The bank in whose van it will arrive will be responsible for the gold until it is placed in the machine. From then on you will accept full responsibility until you obtain a receipt for it from the manager of the Bank of France, in the Place de l'Opéra, Paris. The French bank will send up their van to meet you; it is painted green so that you will be able to recognize it. There will be an official and two gendarmes for escort. You will see the bullion put into the van and accompany it to the bank, where you will be presented with a receipt. The receipt you will bring back here. Is that all quite clear?'

'Perfectly,' replied Biggles. 'I assume the gold will be in those little wooden boxes with rope handles, like the one you showed me the other day?'

'Yes.'

'Just one more question. Does any one outside this room, except the bank officials, know that this shipment is being made?'

'No one. That is, not as far as we know—not that we have any reason to suppose that any one else knows.'

'You would have said the same thing about the previous shipments, I take it—those that went wrong?'

'Why—er—yes; I suppose we should.'

'That's all I wanted to know, thank you. My engines will be ticking over at twelve o'clock,' Biggles promised, as he got up. 'And I shall be back here at six, or thereabouts, with the receipt. Good morning, gentlemen.'

II

At five minutes to twelve Smyth started the engines of the Cormorant. For two or three minutes he allowed

27

them to warm up, and then, with his eyes on the instrument board, he opened the throttle slowly to its limit. Satisfied that the engines were giving their full revolutions, he climbed down and walked round to the nose of the machine to where Biggles, Algy, and Ginger, dressed in flying kit, were standing.

'So you didn't say anything about your going to see Raymond?' Algy was saying.

'No,' replied Biggles. 'It would only have led to long explanations. Naturally, Cronfelt would have wanted to know what Raymond said, and so on, and on this jaunt I don't propose to tell any one outside ourselves what anybody said, in so far as it relates to plans. Once started, I should have had to tell him about acquiring an old R.A.F. Bulldog* fighter for escort purposes, and how Raymond wangled us a couple of machine-guns, and all the rest of it. After all, that's our affair, not Cronfelt's; I warned him I should run things my own way, anyway. I want to keep this escort business dark. No one must see the machine on the ground, so no one must be allowed in the hangar. The door must be kept locked, except when we are moving machines in and out. Now that we have fixed up living quarters in the hangar somebody will always be there, so no one can get in without our knowing it.'

'I wouldn't have flown otherwise,' declared Algy. 'The only aspect of this show that scares me is the thought of any one tampering with the machines. Structural failure in the air is something no man—'

'All right, laddie, that's enough of that sort of talk,' broke in Biggles. 'We've decided never to leave the

---

* Single-seat fighter with twin machine-guns synchronized to fire through the propellor.

hangar unguarded, so I don't think we need worry on that score. Hello, this looks like our cargo arriving,' he went on quietly, with his eyes on the gate.

A dark-painted, closed van drew in, ran smoothly along the tarmac, and pulled up beside the waiting aeroplane. A door in the back opened and three men stepped out. The first, in civilian clothes, came towards the pilots, while the other two, in sober uniforms, began pulling out a number of small, but obviously very heavy boxes.

'Major Bigglesworth?' inquired the civilian.

Biggles stepped forward.

'I'm Grant from the South Central Bank. My instructions are to deliver these boxes to you. Will you kindly sign this receipt?'

Biggles counted the boxes as one by one they were placed on the floor of the cabin. When the tally was complete he signed the receipt form and handed it back to the bank official, who, with a word of thanks, returned to the car.

Two men in dark clothes and bowler hats stepped out from the side of the hangar, and after a friendly nod to Biggles, got into the car, which was backed clear of the slipstream.

Biggles watched it go with a queer expression on his face. 'Those two fellows must be detectives,' he said quietly to Algy. 'But they might have been a couple of gunmen for all we knew. I didn't see them standing there, did you? Nor did I see them arrive.'

Algy shook his head. 'No, I didn't see them, either,' he confessed.

'Which should be a lesson to us. We shall have to keep a sharper look-out,' observed Biggles grimly, as he turned towards the Cormorant. 'Now, laddie, you know what to do,' he went on quietly. 'Keep us in sight, but don't get too close. I don't want anybody to suspect that you are acting as escort. If you see another machine coming towards us, come right in and act as circumstances suggest best. Without knowing what is likely to happen, I can't advise any particular line of action if anything does happen. Use your own judgement. Come on, Ginger, let's be going.'

'Funny, isn't it?' he continued, as they climbed into their seats. 'No more formality than if we were taking over a crate of eggs. I expected some sort of parade, with a band playing and all the rest of it.'

He felt for the throttle. The machine moved slowly over to the far side of the aerodrome, turned into the wind, and at a signal from the control tower, rose gracefully into the air, afterwards turning in a wide circle until her nose was pointing south.

It was a perfect flying day, without a bump* in the air or a cloud in the sky. Not another machine was in sight.

For twenty minutes the Cormorant flew on. The wide expanse of Ashdown Forest came into view, but soon gave way to the curious regular pattern of the Kentish hopfields. Presently the Channel loomed up like a low, dark blue cloud, and in obedience to a signal from Biggles, Ginger left his seat and disappeared into the cabin. But he was back before the coastline of France appeared.

'Can you see him?' asked Biggles.

'Yes. At least, I can see a machine on our quarter, about two thousand feet above us. It's about three miles away, flying in the same direction as ourselves.'

* A local disturbance of air currents causing rough or uneven flying.

'Yes. That'll be Algy right enough,' declared Biggles. 'Any one else in sight?'

'Can't see anything else.'

'Good enough. Keep your eyes skinned for strangers, all the same. If you see another machine, let me know.'

'O.K., Chief,' returned Ginger, as he settled himself once more in his seat.

They were passing over the long, multi-coloured, hedgeless fields of northern France now. Several times Biggles relinquished control to Ginger and scrutinized the sky carefully, section by section, paying particular attention to that part which was more or less cut off by the blinding rays of the sun; but with the exception of the one tiny speck far above and behind them, not a mark of any sort broke the cloudless blue of the sky.

The time passed slowly, as it always does in the air when there is no incident to break the smooth, swift rush through space. The long, narrow fields began to give way to small market gardens and isolated groups of houses, while in the distance the dull haze that always hangs over big towns marked the position of the French capital. Once Biggles started as three machines swept down out of the haze, but it was only a formation of French military machines, and he smiled at Ginger as they roared away towards their unknown destination.

'Well, here we are,' he observed, as Le Bourget came into view. 'All very simple, wasn't it?'

'Yes,' agreed Ginger. 'If we never have any more trouble than this, we shan't have much to worry about.'

Biggles throttled back, glided past the control tower, and on receiving permission to land, touched his wheels gently in the centre of the aerodrome, afterwards taxiing slowly to that area of the tarmac reserved for arrivals. 'Take a look and see if you can see Algy,' he ordered.

Ginger stood up. 'Yes,' he said quickly. 'He's coming in.'

'Good,' replied Biggles. 'Meet him as soon as he lands. You know what you are to do.'

'Yes.'

'That looks like my barrow over there,' continued Biggles, pointing to a dark-green painted van with three men in uniform standing beside it looking in the direction of the British machine.

'Two of them are gendarmes, anyway,' replied Ginger, as Biggles taxied up close to the van and switched off his engines.

One of the men stepped forward while the other two followed slowly. 'Major Bigglesworth?' he inquired in perfect English.

'Yes, you expected me, I think,' answered Biggles.

'That is correct. I am of the Bank of France; here are my credentials. The car is waiting.' He handed Biggles a small leather wallet with a seal attached.

Biggles read the document carefully and handed it back. 'Very well, m'sieur,' he said. 'Everything seems to be in order; here is the cargo.'

Assisted by the driver of the car, the bullion boxes were swiftly transferred to the van under the watchful eyes of the gendarmes and the curious stares of two or three mechanics and aerodrome officials. The driver took his place at the wheel; the bank official sat beside him, while the two gendarmes entered the back of the van and sat on the side seats with the boxes at their feet. Automatically Biggles followed, seating himself opposite to them, and making himself comfortable for the tiring forty minutes ride through the narrow traffic-thronged streets that led to the centre of the city and their destination. The door slammed and the van glided forward easily.

Now it is a fact beyond dispute that many pilots develop a curiously alert sense of direction, rudiments possibly of the same faculty that the carrier pigeon possesses to such a remarkable degree. Biggles was no exception, as he had proved on more than one occasion when thick weather had obliterated all signs of the earth—an unpleasant state of affairs which did not, however, prevent him from reaching his objective. On the ground this feeling of direction was not so acute, but it still existed in a modified form, and it was no doubt due to this that there began to form in his mind an uneasy sensation that the driver of the van was not following the main road to Paris. The only window was in the rear of the van, set in the door, and it was too high up for him to see out without standing up. The feeling first occurred when the vehicle had been on the move for about a quarter of an hour or so, and they should, according to his calculations, have passed the Coty works, the factory where the world-famous perfumes are made. Subconsciously, he had been looking up at the window, knowing that it would be possible, as they passed it, to see the trade-mark on the top of the building. That they had not passed it he was quite sure, and when, at the end of another five minutes, it had still not come into view he suspected that something was wrong. The car took a sharp turn to the left and doubt became certainty.

Calmly, he stood up and looked out of the window. As he more than half expected, the scene was strange to him. Instead of the busy, stall-lined streets, they were speeding through a narrow slum. He spun round with a glint in his eye, lips parted to demand an explanation; but at the sight that met his eyes the words died away and a bitter smile spread over his face. Neither of the gendarmes had moved, but in the right hand of each was an automatic, with the muzzle pointing towards him.

He nodded slowly and resumed his seat. 'So that's it, is it?' he said quietly.

'*Oui, m'sieur; c'est ca*,*' replied one of the gendarmes. 'Do as you are told and you will not be hurt. But if—' The man shrugged his shoulders expressively.

Biggles did not reply. To tackle two men armed with automatics, who were covering him at a range of not more than three feet, would have been an act of the sheerest folly. In fiction, or in a screen-picture, something might have been done, but in cold fact, no, and his common sense prevented him from taking steps that could only end in disaster. That they would shoot if he offered resistance he had no doubt whatever, and at such a range they could hardly miss. He bit his lip as he looked at the boxes on the floor and then back at the men. There was nothing he could do. There was nothing he could say.

He wondered where he was being taken, and was contemplating asking the question—not that he expected an answer—when, with a grinding of brakes, the van skidded to a standstill. A moment later the door was thrown open, and the man whom he had assumed to be a bank official appeared. There was a mocking smile on his face as he invited his prisoner to descend.

Biggles had no choice but to comply. He stood up,

* French: Yes, Sir, that is it

but his foot on the step, and was about to step down when a heavy weight struck him in the small of the back. The attack was so utterly unexpected that he was thrown off his balance, and measured his length on the ground. Before he could pick himself up there was a clash of gears; the van leapt forward, and by the time he was on his feet it had swung round the corner and disappeared from sight. He ran swiftly to the point at which it had disappeared, but, as he expected, there was no sign of it, so he looked about him.

He found himself standing in an ordinary suburban street of private houses. There were one or two people in sight, but they paid no attention to him; only a paper-boy with a bicycle, who had evidently witnessed the occurrence, stood on the edge of the pavement laughing at his discomfiture. Biggles walked over to him and spun a two-franc piece in the air. 'Where is the nearest garage?' he said swiftly, in French.

'In the Rue Michelinos, m'sieur,' replied the boy.

'How far away is it?'

'Half a kilometre.'

'Ride there quickly and ask them to send me a car or a taxi. Hurry! I will wait here.'

In a few minutes a taxi whirled round the corner in typically French fashion; a little way behind was the paper-boy, pedalling furiously. Biggles gave him his two francs and jumped into the cab.

'To the Bank of France, Place de l'Opéra,' he directed.

In twenty minutes he was there, and, jumping out, saw Algy and Ginger standing on the pavement beside another taxi. He paid his fare and joined them. 'Don't ask questions; I haven't time to answer them now,' he said tersely. 'They were on the job right enough. Everything all right?'

'Quite O.K.,' replied Algy.

'Fine! Then stand fast.' Biggles hurried into the bank.

It was at once apparent that the robbery was known, for two gendarmes stood on duty at the door, and there were others inside. 'I must see the manager at once,' he told a nervous-looking clerk.

'I am sorry, monsieur, but it is not possible. He is engaged,' was the quick reply.

'Go and tell him that Major Bigglesworth wishes to speak to him.'

The clerk nearly fell off his stool. He took one amazed look and then bolted to the rear. 'This way, monsieur,' he called a minute later.

Biggles walked through to manager's office, where he found the official he sought in earnest conversation with a short, stout man in dark clothes. They both stared at him as he entered. 'Where have they taken it, do you know?' asked the manager bluntly.

Biggles looked puzzled. 'Taken what?' he said.

'The gold.'

'The gold? I don't understand. I have the gold here; will you please accept it and give me a receipt.'

The manager staggered back, while a frown furrowed the forehead of the other man, who stepped forward and tapped Biggles lightly on the chest. 'Allow me to present myself,' he said. 'Detective Boulanger, of the Paris Sûreté*.'

'Pleased to meet you, sir,' replied Biggles. 'What can I do for you?'

* The French Criminal Investigation Department.

'This robbery—'

'What are you talking about? There has been no robbery.'

'The detective looked at the manager. 'What is this?' he snapped.

The manager ran his hands through his hair. 'But the van was taken,' he said. 'The driver and the gendarmes who were to act as escort were kidnapped. The driver has rung up to say—'

'I'm sorry, but I know nothing about that,' interrupted Biggles. 'I've brought the gold along in a taxi. It is waiting outside. May I suggest that it is brought into the bank? You'll find my assistants with it.'

The manager departed quickly, and Biggles turned to find the detective regarding him quizzically.

'Young man, you know more about this affair than you pretend,' he observed shrewdly.

'Yes,' answered Biggles. 'And in fairness to you, I will tell you what happened. In fairness to me, will you please regard the matter as confidential? You must take any steps you think proper, of course, but it would be better from my point of view if the story was withheld from the newspapers. That will leave the—er—crooks wondering what is going on.'

A look of understanding came into the detective's eyes. 'Ah-ha! Quite so, m'sieur,' he said quietly.

'You see,' explained Biggles, 'I shall probably run into them again one day. They work in the dark. We, too, will work in the dark.'

'Precisely! It shall be as you say.'

Briefly, Biggles told him what had happened, and was just finishing as the manager returned; his face was beaming.

'All in order,' he cried. 'Here is the receipt. I have not yet rung up your firm in London; I must do so—'

'Please do nothing of the sort,' broke in Biggles, glancing at the receipt and putting it into his pocket. 'I am returning immediately, and will make my report in person. If you use the telephone some one may overhear, and I would prefer that those who attempted the robbery work things out for themselves. These affairs have had too much publicity in the past. Monsieur Boulanger will explain what I mean.'

'Very well, m'sieur, it shall be as you say.'

'Thank you. Good day, gentlemen.'

The detective looked curiously after Biggles' retreating form; then he turned to the manager and winked. 'He is no fool, that one,' he muttered. 'We shall hear of him again, I fancy!'

III

At ten minutes past five Biggles opened the door of Stella Carstairs' office. He was humming softly to himself, but he broke off when he saw her for her face was pale and her eyes suspiciously red. 'Why, what's the matter, Miss Carstairs?' he said quickly.

'So they got it after all,' she replied, looking at him miserably.

'Got what?'

'The gold.'

Biggles inclined his head. 'Who told you that?' he asked softly.

'Who told me? The story is all over the City. Haven't you seen the newspapers?'

'To tell the truth, I haven't.'

Stella beckoned him towards the window. 'Look,' was all she said.

Biggles walked swiftly to the window and looked down. On the opposite side of the road a newsboy's placard displayed in bold type the words

'ANOTHER GREAT GOLD ROBBERY.'

'It looks as if they're speaking out of their turn,' he observed.

Stella sprang to her feet. 'Do you mean to say that the gold has not been stolen?' she gasped.

'I delivered the gold to the bank and have the receipt in my pocket, so I don't see how it can be,' replied Biggles casually.

Stella sat down suddenly and laughed a trifle hysterically.

Biggles bent forward; his face was very serious. 'Tell me,' he said, 'do you know who started this story?'

'No. Somebody rang up, from the Stock Exchange, I think, and told my father. He is terribly upset. You see, every one in the City knows what the loss would mean to this firm, and our shares have slumped, which means that as they stand now my father is ruined. The ten-pound shares in Cronfelt & Carstairs, which were worth eight pounds this morning, have fallen to five pounds—and they are still falling. I've been watching them on the tape machine. All my father's money—all he has left—is in Cronfelt & Carstairs.'

'When it is known that there has been no robbery the shares will recover,' answered Biggles. 'Listen,' he went on swiftly. 'Have you authority to buy shares in your father's name?'

'Of course.'

'Then ring up your brokers and buy five thousand

shares at the lowest price. Get going. If somebody is trying to bust your firm, and that's what it looks like to me, they are due for a shock. I'll talk to you again later on. I must go now.'

He walked through into the inner office. Cronfelt was sitting with his elbows on his desk and his chin in his hands; Carstairs was slumped in an armchair staring unseeingly into the fire, but they both sprang up when they saw him.

'You here!' gasped Cronfelt.

Biggles tossed his hat into a chair and sat down in another. 'Certainly,' he replied. 'Why not? I'm a few minutes late I'm afraid, but I was delayed by the traffic.'

'Well, it's a bad business,' returned Cronfelt sombrely. 'I'm sorry, Bigglesworth, sorry for your sake—'

'Don't ever be sorry for me, sir,' interrupted Biggles shortly. 'What are you talking about, anyway?'

'This robbery—the gold.'

Biggles frowned. 'There's a lot of talk going on about a robbery,' he said slowly. 'Too much, in fact. I should like to know where it started. Who told you there had been a robbery, Mr. Cronfelt?'

'But every one knows of it.'

'Funny how these rumours get about, isn't it? Looks as if some one expected a robbery but was a bit premature, eh?'

'Stop talking in riddles,' cried Carstairs. 'How did they get it?'

'They didn't,' Biggles told him, and tossed the receipt on the desk. 'The gold went straight to the Bank of France.'

The two men stared at him in a hush in which

the ticking of the clock on the mantlepiece sounded curiously loud.

Cronfelt was the first to recover. He picked up the receipt, stared at it, and then at Biggles. 'Will you please tell us all you know about this alleged robbery,' he said briskly.

Biggles thought for a moment. 'Yes,' he said quietly, 'I suppose I had better, although you will remember that I warned you that I do not like disclosing my plans. In this case, however, you have a right to know. It was all very simple. You see, my responsibility for the gold did not begin until it was put into my machine. I took precautions to make sure that nothing could happen to the machine on the ground, and further safeguards to prevent interference in the air. Any attempt at a robbery would therefore have to be made over the other side. An attempt *was* made. It so happens, however, that there is a false bottom to the fuselage of my machine—a little matter I arranged with the makers before delivery. When I started there were a number of boxes in the secret compartment—we'll call it that—each one identical with those containing the gold. They were filled with lead. In the air, my assistant reversed the position of the boxes. Those filled with lead were stacked in the cabin, and the gold was put into the false bottom. When I arrived at Bourget, those containing lead were pulled out and put into the bank van. After it had departed, the real boxes were taken out by my assistants, put into a taxi, and driven to the bank to await my arrival. Which was a good thing, because the bank van had been commandeered by the crooks, who now find themselves in possession of a nice little lot of metal normally used for the manufacture of gas-pipes. That's all there was to it.'

'But my dear Bigglesworth, what you did was most irregular. Suppose—'

'Well, suppose what?'

'Fancy putting all that gold into an ordinary taxi! You might have lost the lot.'

'You're dead right, I might—very easily,' agreed Biggles emphatically. 'As it happens, I didn't, so I don't see what you've got to complain about.'

'I'm not complaining, but as a business man—'

'Business, my eye,' snapped Biggles. 'It's not by adopting regular business methods that we shall outwit these crooks. They understand those. It's the irregular ones that will baffle them.'

'The Insurance people would raise a nice storm if they knew about it.'

'I imagine they'd have raised a bigger storm if the gold had been pinched,' retorted Biggles. 'Who's going to tell them about it, anyway; are you?'

'No,' replied Cronfelt slowly. 'But you can't pull off a trick like that more than once,' he added. 'Next time the crooks will ransack the machine for the real stuff.'

'With your permission we'll leave next time until it happens, shall we? May I point out that I've done what I was asked to do, so these discussions as to what might have happened, or what might happen in the future, are all very futile.'

Carstairs sprang up. 'By Jove!' he cried, 'I've just remembered. You've saved us, Bigglesworth, and I for one am grateful, for they were hammering the firm to pieces on the Stock Exchange.'

'Yes, by heaven,' cried Cronfelt. 'I'd forgotten that. This is where we step in and make a nice profit.' He darted to the tape machine, but after one look he swung round with a queer expression on his face. 'This is very odd,' he said in a hard voice. 'Half an hour ago our shares were down to five pounds; now they've jumped up to over eight. It must be known that there's been no robbery. Have you told anybody, Bigglesworth?'

'I mentioned it to Miss Carstairs as I came through her office, that's all. Personally, I don't see why the fact that there hasn't been a robbery shouldn't be known just as quickly as the rumour that there had been one. A lot of people seem to be taking an interest in your affairs, Mr. Cronfelt.'

Carstairs had rung the bell, and all three men turned as Stella came in.

'Have you told any one what Bigglesworth told you as he came in?' inquired Cronfelt, before her father could speak.

'Not a soul.'

'Have you seen the tape?'

'Yes.'

'Then you've seen that our shares have jumped from five pounds to more than eight pounds? Can you account for that?'

'Yes, I think so,' answered Stella frankly. 'On the strength of what Major Bigglesworth told me I rang up my father's brokers and bought five thousand shares at bottom price. I assume that the Stock Exchange realized from that, that the robbery was only a rumour; hence the soaring price. I was tempted to sell out again at eight pounds, which would have shown a profit on the deal of fifteen thousand pounds, but on second thoughts I decided to hold on to them and leave the decision to my father.'

'That's splendid,' cried Carstairs delightedly.

Biggles stood up. 'Well, gentlemen, if that's all I'll be getting along,' he said. He turned to Cronfelt, who was looking at him with an extraordinary expression on his face. 'By the way, Mr. Cronfelt,' he added, 'you haven't told me yet who told you there had been a robbery.'

'Why, what does it matter?'

'Oh, it's just a matter of interest,' replied Biggles lightly.

'It was the manager of the Bank of France, of course. Naturally, he rang me up at once.'

'Ah,' breathed Biggles. 'He would—of course. I'd forgotten that.'

'I begin to perceive that Colonel Raymond did not exaggerate your qualities,' Cronfelt called after him as he went towards the door.

'Oh, and by the way,' smiled Biggles, ignoring the double-sided remark, 'our friends who snaffled the lead are likely to regret it.'

'Why?'

'There is an ounce of ammonal* fixed inside the lid of each of the stolen boxes. The lad who pulls the first one open is likely to take a short flight through the roof.'

Cronfelt started, and a heavy frown settled on his face. 'What!' he cried. 'Good gracious, Bigglesworth, you can't do things like that.'

'Can't I? You don't know me yet.'

'But that's barbarous.'

'Not at all. We didn't invite them to take the boxes, did we? People who take what doesn't belong to 'em can't very well complain if the thing doesn't turn out to be what they thought it was, can they? My idea was to discourage them from meddling with our belongings.

* A high explosive

44

Get 'em guessing. Nothing like rattling the enemy, you know. You can get me on the 'phone if you want me — goodbye.'

As he rang for the lift a hand was laid on his arm, and turning he looked into the face of Stella.

'Thank you,' she said quietly. 'I'm glad you're working with us, after all, and I shall have more confidence in you in the future,' she smiled.

'That's fine,' returned Biggles, as he stepped into the lift. 'But don't get an exaggerated idea of my ability. This is only the first round, remember.'

Chapter 3
The Second Round

I

At half-past eight the following morning Biggles was going over the Cormorant carefully with Smyth when Algy called to him that Colonel Raymond was on the telephone. Accordingly, he hurried to the small compartment that had been match-boarded off from the rest of the hangar to serve as living accommodation, and picked up the receiver.

'Hello, sir, you're an early bird this morning,' he greeted the Assistant Commissioner of Police.

'It's the early bird that catches the worm, you know,' was the cheerful reply.

'Not always. Sometimes he catches a slug—in the back of the neck,' contradicted Biggles. 'But what's the news?'

'That's what I've rung up to ask you. What happened yesterday?'

'I'll tell you about it sometime, but not over the 'phone.'

'I see. Now look; I've a fellow coming down to see me this morning whom I'm anxious you should meet. Do you mind if I bring him down?'

'I'd rather you didn't come here, if you don't mind,' answered Biggles quickly. 'I don't want anybody to know that I am in direct touch with you.'

'What shall we do about it then?'

'What time is the chap calling on you?'

'Nine-fifteen.'

'Suppose I run up?'

'That would be splendid.'

'Right, sir. I'll be with you about nine-thirty or there-abouts.'

'Excellent; I'll leave instructions for you to be brought straight up to my office. Good-bye.'

'Good-bye, sir.' Biggles hung up the instrument and turned to where the others were regarding him with curiosity.

'What's in the wind now?' asked Algy.

'Nothing important. Raymond wants me to meet some fellow in connexion with this business, I imagine. You'd better stand by while I slip along. If any messages comes through from Cronfelt or Carstairs, ring me at Scotland Yard—Colonel Raymond's office—but don't tell any one where I am.'

'Good enough.'

In a few minutes Biggles was on his way, and shortly before the arranged hour he steered his Bentley out of Whitehall into the courtyard of the famous police headquarters. A constable, who had evidently been on watch for him, took him at once to the Assistant Commissioner's office.

Colonel Raymond shook hands cordially, and then introduced him to a small, neatly dressed man who was looking at him with undisguised interest.

'I want you to meet Sir Guy Brunswick,' he said. 'Brunswick, this is Major Bigglesworth.'

'Good morning, sir,' said Biggles, shaking hands.

'Sir Guy, by the way, is head of the General Transportation Insurance Corporation,' explained the Colonel.

Biggles started slightly. 'I see,' he answered slowly, wondering vaguely how such an insignificant-looking man could hold down such a responsible position. But when Sir Guy spoke, he knew, for there was a steely quality in his voice that revealed a shrewd, purposeful character.

'I don't think we need beat about the bush, Bigglesworth,' he began. 'We are the insurance brokers to the firm for whom you are working, but Colonel Raymond knows that our interest in these gold shipments is national as well as financial. We have watched the sequence of events leading up to the present position with interest, as you will have no difficulty in believing. We have been faced with difficulties, very great difficulties, but now, with you on our side, we believe that things are shaping the way we want them to go. You see, your present employment is not due to chance.' A ghost of a smile flitted across the speaker's rather pale face. 'It was I who suggested to Carstairs that he should consult Colonel Raymond, in order to provide the Colonel, who had already mentioned you to me, with the necessary excuse to introduce you into the—er—scheme.'

'Sounds like a neat little plot,' observed Biggles.

'Call it that if you like. We—'

'One moment, sir, before you go any further,' broke in Biggles. 'I hope you are not going to suggest that I act in any way detrimental to the interests of my employers, or put over what is aptly called in the United States a "doublecross" by divulging to you, or any one else, the inside activities of our business.'

Sir Guy Brunswick threw a swift glance at Colonel Raymond.

'Either I work for them, or I don't,' went on Biggles

bluntly. 'If I do, then nobody else comes into the picture.'

'Quite right. Naturally,' replied Sir Guy Brunswick, rather uncomfortably. 'All I want to tell you is this. The Colonel here does not altogether agree with me, but I believe—nay, I am sure—that these gold robberies are part of a scheme of far greater magnitude than you suspect. Raymond thinks that they are being carried out for personal gain. I prefer to believe that they have their root in the very foundation of some European Power, for gold is king, and a nation without gold in its cellars to-day is in a sorry plight. Every nation in the world is out to collect gold, by fair means if possible, but there may be one or two who are not particular as to the means they employ to acquire it. They would stoop to *any* means.'

'Why not say foul means, and have done with it?'

'I will. Foul means.'

Biggles rubbed his chin thoughtfully for a moment or two. 'Maybe you're right,' he said looking up. 'But what has that got to do with me?'

'Just as much as you like to make it,' replied Brunswick sharply. 'Now listen, Bigglesworth; I'll tell you what I'm prepared to do, and you can please yourself what you do about it. Run this gang of crooks to earth, or point out to me the man who is at the head of it—or the chief operator in this country—and I'll make you a present of a cheque for ten thousand pounds. That is a personal matter between ourselves. To that sum my firm will add another five thousand.'

Biggles drew a deep breath. 'That's a lot of money,' he said quietly.

'It is, but if it ever finds its way into your pocket you

will have earned it, if I know what I'm talking about,' returned Brunswick grimly.

'Well, we'll see what we can do about it. If—' Biggles broke off as the telephone whirred sharply.

'It's for you, Biggles,' said the Colonel, after he had picked up the receiver.

Biggles took the instrument from him. 'Yes? Oh, it's you, Algy. What's the trouble? . . . I see . . . I'll be right along . . . Cheerio.' He rose and picked up his hat. 'I must get back,' he said. 'I've a little matter to attend to right away,' he added, turning towards the door.

'Yes, I had an idea Parkinson's Bank might ask Cronfelt & Carstairs if you could take a shipment over for them to-day,' said Brunswick quietly, selecting a cigarette from his case.

Biggles swung round, frowning. 'You seem to be very well informed, sir,' he said coldly.

'So I ought to be, considering we are insuring the bullion,' returned the baronet brightly. 'I suppose you know that your employers have circulated the leading London bankers and bullion brokers to the effect that their subsidiary company, Biggles & Co., are open to accept charters of gold and precious stones?'

'No, I didn't know that.'

'Then I'm glad to be able to give you some information.'

'As a matter of fact, something of the sort was part of the original arrangement, so there was no reason why they shouldn't,' declared Biggles.

'I didn't say there was, did I?'

'It's a big consignment, I understand?' went on Biggles, ignoring the thrust.

'We've covered just over thirty thousand pounds'

worth of gold; the insurance was effected late last night.'

Biggles nodded. 'I see,' he said softly. 'Well, I'll see about moving it. Good-day, sir—keep your cheque-book handy. Good-bye, Colonel; I'll let you know if anything important transpires.'

'And let me know if you want any help,' replied Raymond anxiously. 'Don't underestimate this gang; remember, you don't know who you are up against.'

Biggles threw him a curious smile. 'Perhaps you're right,' he said quietly as he went out of the door, 'but I have an idea.'

II

As he drove though the aerodrome gates he met a private van coming out, and guessed that the bank had delivered the shipment of metal.

'You've been a long time,' growled Algy, as Biggles pulled up sharply in front of the hangar, near to where the Cormorant was standing with propellors ticking over.

'Yes, I know,' replied Biggles morosely. 'I was longer with Raymond than I thought I should be, and every blessed traffic signal was against me coming back. No matter; we're all ready to start, eh?'

'No, as a matter of fact, we're not,' Algy told him. 'There's been a mistake. The bank rang up in a bit of a panic just now to say that one of the bullion boxes had been left behind by accident. Apparently the packers found that the ingots wouldn't go into the specified number of boxes; there was one over, so they've put it in a box by itself, and are rushing it down by a special car; but they told me to tell you that you can please yourself whether you wait for it or not. It isn't vitally important, so if the delay is likely to cause inconvenience, we can go without the odd box.'

'I see, but we may as well wait. How long since they rang up?'

'About twenty minutes or so. The car had already left, so it should be here any minute now.'

'Good enough; I'll slip my things on. I don't like hanging about with all this gold on board, so don't leave it—keep your eyes on it.'

'I think we're pretty safe; the bank's taking no chances. Take a look.' So saying, Algy walked over to the Cormorant and opened the cabin door.

Sitting in the seats were two uniformed policemen.

Biggles nodded to them and closed the door again. 'You're satisfied they're—what they look like?' he inquired sharply.

'You bet your life I am. As a matter of fact, the bank told me that two policemen had been detailed to accompany the gold and stand by it until we were in the air. They were inside the van when it came; locked in with it. The bank official who brought the Bill of Lading told me they were locked in when the last box of gold was put inside; he had to unlock the door to let them out.'

'O.K., laddie. That's good enough. Hello, this looks like the other box arriving.'

A Daimler saloon had swung round the corner and was heading straight for the waiting aeroplane.

'Major Bigglesworth, sir?' inquired the driver respectfully, as the car pulled up with a jerk.

'Yes,' answered Biggles.

'I have a box to deliver to you; will you please sign for it?'

Biggles glanced at the box, saw it was sealed with the bank seal, signed for it, and watched it put aboard with the others. Then he put on his flying-jacket and climbed into the cockpit.

'Engines O.K., sir,' called Smyth.

'Then tell the coppers they can get out—unless they feel like a trip to Paris.'

But the policemen laughingly got out and watched the machine sail serenely into the air.

'Is Algy following us?' Biggles asked Ginger a few minutes later.

Ginger stood up and looked over the tail. 'Yes, he's climbing for height on our starboard quarter,' he answered, and settled himself down for the journey, but keeping a watchful eye on the sky.

The Channel was reached, and the long pointed finger of Dungeness was soon a brown smudge behind them, for as usual Biggles was taking the direct route to the French capital.

Twenty minutes later, with the French coast lying along the Cormorant's port bow, he was about to throttle back a trifle in order to lose some of the altitude he had taken for the sea crossing, when his nostrils twitched suddenly. He looked sharply at Ginger, who sprang up and dived for the door leading to the cabin. He was back in an instant. His face was ashen. 'We're afire,' he screamed.

Biggles snatched one swift glance aft over the side of the cockpit. Great clouds of smoke were pouring from the machine, to be whipped by the propellors into a churning wake which, for a mile or more, marked the course they had taken. But almost before his eyes had conveyed to his brain the full horror of the calamity, he had flung the Cormorant into a steep side-slip, and was dropping like a stone, wing-tip first, towards the bleak expanse of sand that fringed the French foreshore.

'Can you get to the fire extinguishers?' he snapped.

'No! The cabin is full of smoke,' yelled Ginger, who was hanging on to the side of the now vertical cockpit.

'Take over and hold her in the slip,' shouted Biggles above the wailing of the wires, and relinquishing control, he tried to get into the cabin to where the fire extinguishers were secured to the walls. But one glance at the suffocating volume of smoke revealed the futility of such an attempt, so he jumped back into his seat and snatched the stick from Ginger's hands. 'We shall just make it,' he said crisply, looking down at the beach that was apparently soaring up to meet them. 'Get ready to jump when we hit, but don't go too soon.'

Ginger nodded desperately.

For a few seconds neither of them spoke. Biggles was watching the ground, nerves quivering at the protesting shriek of the wind in struts and wires. Once he snatched another quick glance behind, but could see no sign of the dreaded flames which, once they appeared, would, he knew, engulf the machine in an instant. 'I'm going to try to land her; we must save her if we can,' he shouted, looking back at the ground now less than two hundred feet below.

For another second or two he held the Cormorant in the side-slip, and then eased her out of it gently. 'Don't jump unless I tell you,' he grated through set teeth. There was neither time nor room to turn into the wind, so he did not attempt it; instead, he dropped the machine on to the sand in the best one-wheel, cross-wind landing he had ever made. Even in the circumstances Ginger was able to appreciate the superb exhibition of airmanship.

Before the machine had stopped running Biggles had switched off the engines and, kicking on top rudder, brought her round into the wind. 'Come on,' he yelled, and leapt to the ground. Automatically he made for the door of the cabin, but the dense cloud of smoke that instantly poured out drove him back. 'Where the dickens is Algy?' he snapped glancing round the sky.

'I was wondering that; can't see him anywhere,' replied Ginger, unfastening his jacket with trembling fingers.

Suddenly Biggles sprang back, enlightenment dawning on his face as he sniffed the pungent reek of smoke. 'I've got it,' he yelled. 'By heaven, they've done us! It's stannic chloride*. Watch out!' He spun round on his heel, with his right hand groping in his pocket for his revolver and eyes questing danger.

There was no need to look far. Racing down the hard, sandy beach at terrific speed was a big, open touring car in which four or five men were crouching forward. The man beside the driver was half standing, balancing a wicked-looking machine-gun on the windscreen. Even as Biggles saw it a burst of flame leapt from the muzzle, and little spurts of sand leapt into the air around the still smoking machine. A bullet caught the loose folds of his flying jacket and almost threw him over backwards, but he recovered, and placing the machine between him and the approaching car, streaked for the low chalk cliffs that bordered the beach at that point. 'Come on!' he yelled. 'Never mind that, you young fool,' he snarled as Ginger whipped out his revolver and half turned to face the car. 'You can't

* A toxic ingredient, hydrochloric acid and tin oxide, giving off pungent white fumes of smoke.

fight a machine-gun with a pistol,' he panted as they darted round a bend in the cliff and sprinted for a place where an opportune landslide offered a path to the top.

Several bullets whistled around them as they scrambled up the ascent, but the shooting, made from a moving vehicle, was wild, and they flung themselves over the crest unscathed. 'Keep your head down,' ordered Biggles, as he flung himself flat and, revolver in hand, began to creep back towards the edge of the cliff. But by the time he reached it he saw to his surprise that the car was already returning over its tracks. One of the men in the back seat, who still wore a gas-mask, waved a mocking salute. The distance was nearly two hundred yards, too far for accurate revolver shooting, so Biggles thrust the revolver back into his pocket and turned his eyes to the machine. It appeared to be exactly as they had left it except that a small wooden bullion box, from which smoke was still pouring, lay outside on the sand.

'They're a smart lot, Ginger,' he muttered thoughtfully, as he began to climb back down the landslide to the beach. 'Let's go and see just how smart they've been.'

One glance told him all he needed to know. The bullion boxes that had been stacked in the cabin were still in place, but the floor of the fuselage had been ripped up, showing the secret compartment. It was empty.

'It's plain enough to see through the thing now,' he continued. 'That last box, supposed to be sent down by the bank, wasn't sent down by the bank at all. It was a plant. The box contained a smoke bomb timed to operate as we approached the French coast. We were bound to act as we did; they could gamble on that with certainty. The first thing any pilot would do, supposing his machine to be on fire, would be to make for the ground. Which is just what we did. They had a car waiting and the rest was easy. Maybe they had two or three cars scattered along the coast. From the cliffs they could see the machine a long way out to sea, see the smoke start, spot the place for which we were making, and speed towards it. Nothing could be more simple. Well, it's no use talking about it, although it would be interesting to know just how they knew the exact position of the secret compartment. They don't appear to have damaged the machine; there was no point in that, although I fancy that if they had caught us they would have made a bonfire of it—with us inside. As it was, we got up the cliff where the car couldn't follow, so they contented themselves with grabbing the cargo and bolting.'

'Hark! Here comes Algy by the look of it,' he went on as a small machine appeared, racing low over the beach. 'He's a bit late on the scene. But never mind about him; get the engines going, Ginger; the crooks might come back, and we don't want to be caught napping.'

Obediently Ginger climbed up into the cockpit just as Algy, who had pulled up in a steep climbing turn when he saw the machine on the ground, whirled round and landed.

'Where the dickens have you been?' asked Biggles as he came up.

'I went for help of course. I saw you going down in flames and never dreamed for a minute that you'd reach the shore. It was no use my trying to get down in the sea beside you in a land-plane, so I tore along to the nearest coastguard station and told them to send out a patrol boat. As it happens, they saw you going down, and there was one already on the way. But what's happened?'

'Can't tell you now,' returned Biggles briskly. 'We had a smoke bomb on board, that's all. Listen! Less than five minutes ago the crooks went off down the beach—look, you can see their tracks—in a big, open touring car. There can't be many cars like that about here; get after them as fast as you can, and if you spot them, follow them. Hang on until you run out of petrol if necessary. But keep some distance off. Don't let them suspect you're watching them. If we can locate their headquarters we might be able to fetch them a crack. If they go to a house, land, find out where it is, and ring me up at the bank in Paris. If you can't get me, ring Detective Boulanger at Police Headquarters and tell him. Off you go.'

Without another word Algy ran back to the Bulldog and skimmed into the air on his quest.

Biggles climbed into the cockpit beside Ginger, took off, and without further incident, landed at Le Bourget fifty minutes later. There was no sign of the expected van, but inquiries revealed that it had been there, had waited for some time, and then, as the aeroplane did not put in an appearance, it had gone away. Biggles at once rang up the bank. It took him some moments to convince the manager that he was actually at Le Bourget, but once that was achieved the van, with an escort of gendarmes, was promised forthwith.

'Apparently the newspapers have got hold of a rare old story this time,' grinned Biggles when he returned to the machine. 'Several coastguards must have seen us go down, and they're not to be blamed if they thought we were falling in flames. We thought so ourselves, if it comes to that. Anyway, several lifeboats put out, but returned and reported they could find nothing, not even a bit of wreckage. Consequently we're reported lost at sea—so the bank manager tells me. The newspapers got hold of the story, of course, learnt the identity of our machine from the English side, and made a front page splash about our presumably untimely end. I could hear the bank manager fairly gasp when I told him who I was.'

After nearly half an hour's wait the van appeared. This time there was no mistake, and in due course, after deriving some amusement from a newspaper, lent to him by one of the gendarmes, Biggles was shown into the manager's office. He found him sitting by the telephone with his hand over the mouthpiece.

'Your office is on the telephone,' he said. 'I have astounded them by telling them that I expect you here at any moment, so they're hanging on the line to have a word with you. Will you please speak?'

Biggles took the receiver. 'Hello,' he called. 'Hello—oh, it's you Mr. Cronfelt. Yes, it's Bigglesworth here. Yes, we are all quite well, thank you. The gold? Yes, that's here, too; I'm just handing it over to the bank. Yes, we had a little affair *en route* . . . The crooks? Oh, they'll be able to make themselves some more gas-pipes. You see, this time we left the gold in the cabin and put the dummies in the secret compartment . . . What's that? Yes, I'm afraid they'll be a bit disappointed . . . of course . . . Yes, I'll be back as soon as I can. Good-bye.'

He turned to find Police Detective Boulanger leaning against the mantlepiece regarding him with a curious smile. His head was nodding up and down, slowly, like a mechanical toy. 'So you—how do you say?—pulled him off again, eh?' he said quietly.

A grin spread slowly over Biggles' face. 'Yes,' he said, 'it looks as if we've won the second round.'

But when an hour had passed and there was still no word from Algy the grin had given place to an anxious frown. Another hour passed, and another, and he began to pace up and down. The afternoon wore on; the bank closed its doors and he had no option but to go out into the street, still without the expected message.

'I don't like the look of it a bit,' he muttered to Ginger, as they sat under the awning of a café and ordered tea. 'I've got a feeling that things have come unstuck somewhere.'

He went to a telephone booth and rang up the control tower at Le Bourget, but the operator could tell him nothing of a small British aeroplane. He tried the Aero Club of France, and the offices of the leading newspapers, but without success. In desperation he rang up Boulanger at the Sûreté. But there was no news of a British aeroplane other than the regular services.

'Tell me monsieur,' he asked Boulanger, 'if a British machine had forced-landed anywhere in France, would it be reported to you?'

'To our International Department here, certainly,' was the prompt reply. 'Unless, of course, it crashed unseen in a forest,' added the detective.

'I see. Many thanks, m'sieur,' replied Biggles, and hung up the receiver.

'Well?' inquired Ginger anxiously, as he rejoined him on the pavement.

Biggles shook his head. 'Nothing doing,' he said.

'What are we going to do?'

'To tell you the truth, I haven't got the foggiest idea,'

Biggles told him. 'Still, it's no use staying here. We might as well get back to our own aerodrome. If Algy is all right, sooner or later he'll find his way home. Moreover, he might get on the telephone, in which case he'll ring us up there, not here, now that he knows the bank is closed.'

'You've said it,' nodded Ginger. 'Come on, then; let's use the daylight as long as we can.'

Chapter 4
Round Three

I

Shortly after nine o'clock the following morning Biggles reported to the office in Lombard Street, where, in the outer office, he found Stella delighted at his second success. The two partners were jubilant. Cronfelt, in his own heavy way, congratulated him on the ruse he had adopted to safeguard the gold, and declared that it was conclusive evidence that the formation of Biggles & Co. had solved the transport problem.

But Biggles was not so sure. Algy's inexplicable silence left him moody and taciturn; but following his own policy of secrecy he did not disclose the sinister fact even to his employers. If Algy was all right, then there was nothing to worry about; if disaster had overtaken him, then neither Cronfelt nor Carstairs could rectify matters, he reasoned. Further, he realized that if he mentioned the matter to them, he would have to explain where Algy was going in the air in another machine, and the fact that the gold-plane had been escorted by an armed single-seater was something that he preferred not to disclose to anybody. So he said nothing about it, and, after handing over the receipt for the last consignment of gold, he went down to the street and returned to the airport.

'Any news?' he asked, as he pulled up at the door of the hangar.

'Not a word' answered Ginger briefly.

'Have you rung up Boulanger?'

'Yes; I told him I was speaking for you, and he told me to tell you that he had heard nothing. He had caused inquiries to be made, and as a result felt safe in saying that no British machine other than regular airliners had landed in France during the last forty-eight hours.'

'That's pretty grim. It's also very odd. Obviously, then, Algy must have travelled beyond the French frontier. He would just about be able to do it with that extra tank he had fitted.'

Ginger nodded. 'Yes,' he said. 'He could just have reached—Germany, for instance.'

Biggles threw him a sidelong glance. 'Why Germany?'

'I don't know; just a hunch.'

'Maybe you're right, but it's no use guessing,' said Biggles shortly. 'Is the machine all right? I fancy we shall soon need it.'

'Yes; we've repaired the floor of the fuselage and done away with the secret compartment, which wasn't secret any longer.'

'Quite right.'

'Why did you say you thought we should soon be needing the machine?'

'I bought a paper on the way down. The pound is weakening, which means that more gold will be sent out of the country. If that is so, Cronfelt & Co. will soon be on the 'phone, or I'm a Dutchman. To tell the truth, I'm sorry, for two reasons. In the first place, I should have preferred to have hung around in case word comes through from Algy. And secondly, this crook gang will be getting peeved after the way we've diddled them twice in succession. This business is becoming a serious proposition to handle single-handed.'

Ginger looked hurt. 'Single-handed! Don't I count for anything?' he asked disappointedly.

'Of course,' replied Biggles quickly. 'What I meant was, I don't relish the idea of flying without an escort, particularly as I'm unarmed. Perhaps you could . . . wait a minute, let me think,' he concluded, sitting down and staring thoughtfully at the ground. Presently he looked up. 'Do you think you could find your way to Paris—solo?' he asked.

'Of course.'

'Sure of it?'

'Absolutely.'

'Could you find your way by an indirect route—say, hit the coast above Calais, and then fly a compass course to Buc Aerodrome instead of Le Bourget? Buc is quite close to Paris; I'd show it you on the map before you started, of course.'

'Yes, I think I could manage it; anyway, I'd have a good shot at it.'

'I believe you would,' cried Biggles, jumping up. 'Then I've got an idea. We'll diddle the swine again. Come on, laddie.' He led the way to the telephone, but it was ringing before he reached it. He picked up the receiver and cocked an eye at Ginger as a voice began speaking. 'Right-oh . . . yes . . . I'll be ready,' he said, and hung up the instrument.

'As I expected. That was the office on the 'phone,' he went on, looking up. 'It looks as if we're in for a rush hour. Three firms want to make shipments. Two concerns are sending fifteen thousand pounds each, and our people are sending ten thousand pounds in bar gold; altogether quite a nice little parcel. Carstairs says the stuff will be here at twelve noon, so this is where we start and get busy,' he continued, picking up the telephone and putting through a call to Croydon Airport.

'Is that Croydon?' he asked. 'I want to speak to Mr. Lindson, of Consolidated Air Lines, please. . . . Is that you, Lindy? Good, this is Biggles speaking. You've got some Cormorants in your fleet, haven't you? . . . Can you let me have one for the day? . . . Yes . . . quite. No, I'll pick it up at Croydon at about twelve-fifteen if you'll have her ready. Many thanks, old boy.'

There was a grim smile on his face as he pushed the telephone aside and rose to his feet. 'Come on,' he said quickly. 'You're going to make the trip of your life, and take the future of Biggles & Co. in your hands. Forty thousand pounds' worth of gold is going to Paris, and you're going to take it. I'm as certain as I stand here that an attempt will be made to get it, so it seems the right moment for us to try a bit of low cunning. Now! This is the plan.'

Ginger's eyes sparkled. 'O.K.—go ahead, Chief; I'm listening,' he murmured.

'When we get the gold aboard, we take off and fly to Croydon, where we transfer the gold to the standard Cormorant that Lindy has promised to have ready for us. I shall at once take off again and fly our own machine empty to Paris, following the usual route, crossing from Dungeness to Bercke. You'll take the hired machine with the gold, to Paris. Go any way you like, but keep well clear of the usual routes. When you get there, don't land at Bourget; make for Buc. You'll wait there until I come. Don't take your eyes off the gold for an instant. If I don't turn up by five o'clock, or if you don't hear from me before then, get in touch with Boulanger through one of the aerodrome officials, and ask him to come and see you. Tell him just what has happened and ask him to see you safely to the bank. Don't forget to get a receipt. Is that clear?'

'Yes; but why need you take over the empty machine?'

'To draw a red herring across the trail, for one thing. To make the thing look all regular and above board for another. If we pull it off, nobody need know how we did it, least of all our own people, who might not approve of such unorthodox methods. They'd probably think I was raving mad to entrust forty thousand jimmy o'goblins worth of gold to you.'

'But why not let me fly the empty machine?'

'I wish you wouldn't ask so many questions.'

'I know; you think there'll be trouble, and if there is, it'll be the empty machine, looking like the real one, that gets—'

'Another word from you and you're fired,' snapped Biggles. 'You do as you're told.'

'Very well,' replied Ginger obediently.

'That's better. Now let's go and tell Smyth what we've fixed, and arrange something in case Algy turns up or telephones.'

II

When Biggles took off from Croydon in his own Cormorant he was convinced that an attempt would be made to get the gold, particularly in view of the value of the consignment. That the thieves would be aware that the shipment was being made he had no doubt whatever. They had known of the others, so it was extremely unlikely that their informant, whoever he was, would fail to notify them of the movement of an even larger quantity of metal. And added to that was the probability that their recent failures would spur them to more desperate measures.

Yet as he headed south through a lonely sky he began to wonder if, after all, he had not been mistaken, for the machine was flying smoothly, and there appeared to be nothing to occasion the slightest alarm. Once he met an Imperial Airways liner of the Heracles class, homeward bound from the Continent, and he waved a passing greeting to the pilot and the curious passengers whose faces he could see pressed against the windows. The Channel came into sight and faded away under his tail twenty minutes later as he crossed the French coast and put his nose down slightly for the final run to his objective.

Where the other machine came from he did not know, and from the very fact of its cunning approach he knew that the pilot was an experienced air fighter. He was flying over the lonely stretch just north of Beauvais at the time, and his first indication of the presence of another machine was the vicious rattle of a machine-gun at perilously close range.

It may have been the speed at which he acted that saved his life, for before five rounds had been fired he had swung the big machine up in an Immelmann turn*, at the same time searching the air for his attacker.

He saw him at once; a long rakish monoplane

* A manoeuvre to change direction by 180 degrees consisting of a half-roll off the top of a loop. Named after Max Immelmann, the successful German fighter pilot 1914–16 with seventeen victories who was the first to use this in combat.

painted dark brown and obviously built for speed and manœuvrability. Even as he watched, it turned at a surprising angle and zoomed up for another burst. From four places around the engine cowling, stabbing, orange flame revealed the positions of the chattering guns, and he knew it was only a question of time before one of the bullets, now ripping through spruce and fabric behind him, found its mark. He made this mental note quite dispassionately, for he was too experienced at the game to be unduly flurried, and his only real emotion was one of cold anger that he was unable to return the attack.

That the monoplane would outclass the big twin-engined machine was only to be expected, so even had he been armed the fight would have been a very one-sided affair; and at that moment the thought occurred to him that the opposing gang must have been aware of his escort on the previous flights, and knew that he had none on the present occasion.

Without attempting to deceive himself, he knew that there was only one thing to do if he wished to save his life, and that was to land, although had he been carrying the gold he might have acted differently. But he was not, so to persist in his present dodging tactics was to hazard his life unnecessarily. Accordingly, he throttled back and pushed the joystick over to hold the machine in a steep side-slip, the quickest and shortest way to the ground. Then, and not before, did he look down to pick out a suitable landing-place.

He saw at a glance that he was over an unusually difficult piece of country. On the right, the landscape consisted entirely of forest, which spread out to the left in the form of isolated clumps of trees. To make matters worse, the ground was not flat, but rolled away in the long undulating waves of gorse-covered terrain that had brought disaster on the ill-fated *R 101**. There was only one field in which a landing might reasonably be attempted, and his enemies were evidently aware of it, for a motorcar was racing towards the spot. Almost automatically he lifted his nose a trifle with a view to finding another spot farther on, but immediately a burst of bullets made the Cormorant quiver from propeller boss to tail-skid. A glance showed the monoplane sitting tight on his tail, so he resumed his original course and flattened out over the uninviting field.

He knew what was going to happen some seconds before the crash actually occurred, but there was nothing he could do about it. The wind, which he knew from his observations had been blowing at a steady twenty-five to thirty miles an hour, died away at the precise moment that his wheel touched the ground, and with a sort of bitter finality he saw the hedge on the far side of the field racing to meet him. Had there been room he would have opened up again, risking the bullets of his efficient escort, but there was not. Better a minor crash, he reflected, than collision with the tree-tops at high speed, which would have been the inevitable result of an attempt to get off again. At the last moment he switched off the ignition to prevent the risk of fire, and kicked out his foot on the rudder bar in a final attempt to save the machine; but in vain. The Cormorant swerved violently, but instantly a grinding, crunching jar announced the collapse of the undercarriage, which he had asked to carry a terrific strain in a direction other than the one allowed for by the designer. The nose bored into the ground; the still turning pro-

---

* British airship which crashed in Northern France in 1930.

pellers disintegrated in a cloud of flying splinters; the tail swung up, and the machine came to rest in a kind of deathly hush.

Biggles ground his teeth with mortification, for although the crash was not a serious one, the machine was definitely out of action and would remain so for many hours. Further, it would cost a fair sum of money to put it into an airworthy condition again. He was, therefore, in no pleasant mood as he turned to face the pilot of the monoplane who, in a smaller machine, had had no difficulty in getting down, and was now running towards him with a squat automatic in his hand. The car had also pulled up, and two of its three occupants, also carrying automatics, were running towards the crashed machine from the lane in which the car had stopped. The third man was bringing the car in through the gate.

'Will you kindly explain the meaning of this?' Biggles asked, in a cold fury that was certainly not feigned, as they ran up.

'Quit bluffin', Mr. Smart Alick Bigglesworth,' snarled one of the two men who had been in the car. His accent was a curious mixture of American drawl and harsh, low German.

'Look what you've done to my machine,' raged Biggles pointing at the wreck.

'That's nothing to what we'll do to it—and you, if you don't quit gassing,' the man promised him.

'Very well, but if you think you can get away with this sort of thing, you'll find you're very much mistaken,' stormed Biggles. 'What do you think you're doing, anyway? Has war broken out?'

The man who was obviously the leader of the party

looked at him malevolently. 'That bluff doesn't work, Bigglesworth,' he began, but Biggles cut him short.

'Bigglesworth! What are you talking about?' he cried. 'Who's Bigglesworth, anyway?' he inquired coldly, adopting a puzzled frown, and he fancied he saw a flicker of doubt creep into the other's eyes.

The man who had been flying the monoplane said something quickly in German—too quick for Biggles to catch.

'You're right; we don't want to waste time,' replied the original spokesman. 'Get the gold out, Carl.'

'Gold!' Biggles laughed incredulously. 'What! in my machine? You're crazy, the lot of you. What do you think I am, an absconding financier? A travelling pawnbroker, perhaps,' he suggested sarcastically. 'Gold, eh? Well, help yourselves; you're welcome to all you can find.'

'Aw, stop yapping,' snarled the man in a sudden fury; but Biggles knew that his words had not been wasted.

With a dour expression he watched two of the men enter the cabin of the Cormorant, while the leader held him covered with his automatic. Presently one of the two men put his head out of the door, and after a glance at his face, Biggles steeled himself for the coming storm.

'There's nothing here,' said the man, almost apologetically, in German.

'What!' cried the man who had remained outside. 'Are you sure?' His eyes were round with astonishment.

'Certain; we've looked everywhere—close enough to have found a packet of cigarettes.'

'When you've finished mauling my machine about, perhaps you will tell me what all this means,' put in

Biggles. 'You'll have to pay for the damage, you know; it isn't my own machine,' he added.

The man looked at the identification letters on the side of the fuselage and compared them with a note in his pocket-book. 'Whose is it?' he asked gruffly.

'I don't know. I hired it for the day from a firm at Hardwick Airport. Biggles, I think the name was.'

The three men looked at each other, and then with one accord walked towards the car that had bumped its way over the uneven ground to the scene.

'Here, you can't just go and leave me like this,' cried Biggles hotly. 'What are your names? You'll have to pay—'

The leader of the gang swung round with an oath and flourished his revolver. 'You keep your distance until we're on the road,' he snapped menacingly. 'We've nothing against you, but don't probe us too far.'

Biggles shrugged his shoulders helplessly, but chuckled to himself as he heard the leader tell the pilot of the monoplane to get back into the air and watch the Paris route for another machine of the Cormorant type. The others entered the car, which was soon bumping its way down the lane back to the main road.

Biggles watched it go with a half smile on his face, for there was nothing he could do except make his way to the nearest village. This he did, but it took him a good half hour, and another twenty minutes to get in touch over the telephone with the makers of the Cormorant aeroplanes.

'I want you to fly a break-down crew over at once,' he told the manager. 'No, it isn't a write-off, but she needs two new props and a new undercart. The leading edge of one wing-tip is a bit bent; I think that's all. If you can get your men over with spare parts right away, you should be able to fly her over to-morrow and give her a quick overhaul. I shan't be here as I have to go on to Paris.'

He described the exact position of the machine, and then rang off, afterwards arranging with the local gend-arme, for a small consideration, to keep an eye on the crash until the break-down crew arrived.

His next step was to hire a car to take him to Beau-vais railway station, where he bought a ticket for Paris, arriving at the Gare du Nord late in the afternoon. Outside the station he engaged a taxi to take him to Buc Aerodrome, and arrived just as the bullion boxes were being stowed in the bank van under the eyes of Ginger, M. Boulanger, and two plain-clothes policemen.

Ginger greeted him joyfully, but the little French detective eyed him dubiously.

'So you have brought him off again, have you, my cabbage?' he observed. 'But you can't win every time, you know,' he added warningly. 'I think it's time we took a hand in the matter, yes?'

'You can take a hand just as soon as you like,' Biggles told him cheerfully. 'Why not send a squadron of inter-ceptor fighters to meet me next time? I'd be glad of their company, believe me.'

'No, this is work for the police, not the Air Force,' the detective remonstrated.

'I'm not so sure,' returned Biggles thoughtfully.

On the way to the bank, which had been kept open for their reception, he told Boulanger what had occurred. In the circumstances, he felt he could not do less.

The Frenchman sighed when he had finished. 'I'm

afraid it is not in France that we shall find the ring-leaders of this gang,' he observed shrewdly.

'I'm inclined to agree with you,' replied Biggles, as the van pulled up outside the bank.

The gold was quickly unloaded and the usual receipt obtained; and after thanking the detective for his assistance, Biggles returned to Buc, where he found Ginger waiting for him with the hired Cormorant. 'Well, it looks as if we've won the third round,' he smiled as he climbed into the cockpit and prepared to take off for the return flight.

'It does,' agreed Ginger, 'but that doesn't mean that the crooks will be likely to throw the towel into the ring. The time is arriving, I fancy, when they will try and slam you one under the belt.' He little knew the truth of the words he spoke.

Biggles smiled grimly. 'I'm afraid you may be right,' he murmured, as he opened the throttle slowly. 'But we can't very well pack up at this stage on that account.'

III

It was dusk when the Cormorant glided down on the aerodrome at Hardwick, and as he taxied in Biggles was surprised to see a neat black and white three-seater Falcon standing outside the hangar.

'Looks as if we've got visitors,' he said to Ginger, who was staring through the windscreen curiously.

'Yes, it's a girl. I can see her talking to Smyth.'

'A girl! By Jove! you're right. Good gracious, it's Stella Carstairs.'

Ginger threw Biggles a quick look. 'I didn't know you two were on visiting terms,' he remarked suspiciously.

'Neither did I,' declared Biggles, as he switched off. 'Any news?' he asked Smyth quietly, as the mechanic ran up to guide the machine in.

'Not a word, sir.'

'I see. All right. Get the machine in, Smyth, will you. By the way, you haven't said anything to Miss Carstairs about Mr. Lacey?'

'No, sir. As a matter of fact, she only arrived a couple of minutes ago.'

Biggles nodded approval. 'Good evening, Miss Carstairs,' he called as he jumped down. 'What are you doing here?'

'Oh, I'm just out for an evening flip in my machine, as the weather is so fine,' she replied brightly, as she came forward to meet them.

'I didn't know you had a machine.'

'I hadn't until yesterday. I've always wanted one, and after our profitable deal the other day my father has let me have one. Nice, isn't she, although she isn't brand new.'

'So I see,' replied Biggles, looking at the smart little monoplane. 'I thought I knew her; her colour and letters are familiar.'

'Of course they are. She belonged to Mr. Briggs, who broke the Australian record in her last month. She's exactly as she was when he finished the flight—long range tanks, and so on; but I'm having standard fittings installed instead. That's why he let me have her at a low figure. He's going in for something bigger.'

'Ah! of course. Well, it's nice of you to call on us.'

'On the contrary, the pleasure is mine,' she smiled; but suddenly her manner changed. 'Well?' she said abruptly, and Biggles noticed that she was a trifle pale.

'That sounds like a question,' he parried awkwardly.

'What happened?'

'Nothing very much.'

'But the gold?'

'It's in the bank; where else would you expect it to be?'

Stella stared at him in amazement. 'Are you telling the truth?' she cried.

Biggles looked pained. 'My dear Miss Carstairs, what object could I have in departing from the truth?' he complained.

'But the crash. We heard you'd been shot down.'

'How did you hear that?' asked Biggles quickly.

'I don't quite know; I think my father told me. But it's in the newspapers, anyway. This is the third attempt at robbery in a week, and they're fairly wallowing in it. But they're all very vague; nobody seems to know quite what happened, so the reports are very conflicting. The French newspaper correspondents swear your machine was crashed; in fact, there's a photo of it in one of the evening papers.'

'Is that so?' Biggles was genuinely amused, for he could well understand that the reports would be at variance. 'Well, here I am, anyway, complete with receipt,' he continued. 'And that's all that really matters, isn't it?'

'You know, Major Bigglesworth, sometimes you can be a very annoying person,' she told him petulantly.

'I'm sorry about that. But don't let us stand here. Come inside. We're a bit primitive, but quite comfortable.'

'So you won't tell me what happened?' she persisted, following him into the hangar.

'I can't see that it matters,' he protested.

'You'll have to tell my father and Mr. Cronfelt.'

'Shall I? That's all you know about it.'

'They're waiting for you to ring them up.'

'In that case, I suppose, I'd better speak to them.'

'They're not at the office, of course. Will you ring Mr Cronfelt at his private address—here's his number. You needn't ring my father because I shall be able to tell him about it when I get back.'

'Thanks. By the way, where do you park your machine?'

'Heston—why?'

'Because I think you ought to be getting back. It's dusk already, you know.'

'You seem very anxious to be rid of me.'

'Not in the least, but I should be sorry to see you break that nice aeroplane—or your neck, for that matter—trying to make a night landing.'

'Thank you; so thoughtful of you to take *me* into consideration.'

Biggles shrugged his shoulders and looked at Ginger helplessly, for the female mentality was one of the things he did not understand. 'Well, I suppose I'd better give Cronfelt a tinkle,' he muttered, reaching for the telephone; but before his hand touched the instrument, the bell was jangling its unmistakable call. 'Hm, this is Cronfelt calling me, I expect,' he observed, turning to the mouthpiece. 'Hello—yes? Hello,' he called carelessly, and then stiffened suddenly as the casual voice of the operator came over the wire.

'Berlin wants you; speak up, please,' she said casually.

'Right, put them through,' answered Biggles. 'Hello,' he called loudly. 'Biggles & Co., here.'

'May I speak to Major Bigglesworth, please?' said the voice that had spoken to him in his rooms on the eve of his acceptance of Cronfelt's proposition. It was polite, but curt.

'You may; this is Bigglesworth speaking,' answered Biggles shortly.

'Ah, Bigglesworth, good evening—'

'Suppose we cut out all that and get down to business,' suggested Biggles harshly.

'Certainly,' came the instant answer. 'Briefly, then, the position is this. No doubt you are wondering what has happened to your partner, so I've rung you up to set your mind at rest. He is quite safe with us, and will remain so provided you do us a small service in return.'

'Go ahead,' invited Biggles.

'To-morrow morning,' continued the voice, 'you will be asked by your firm to fly a parcel of very valuable diamonds to Amsterdam. If you take them to Amsterdam I'm afraid you'll never see your young friend again; but if, however, you will hand them over to us, we will return him to you as a *quid pro quo*.'

'Just how do you propose that I should hand them over to you?' asked Biggles tersely.

'By flying to Aix-la-Chapelle, landing your aeroplane in the large field two miles south of the town, and handing the stones over to a member of our organization who will be waiting there for you. It is really very simple.'

'And what sort of a story do you suggest that I should tell my firm when I get back?'

'Ah! There I cannot help you; that is a matter you must work out for yourself. But our time is nearly up and we may be cut off at any moment. May we expect to see you to-morrow?'

'You may,' answered Biggles coolly.

'Thank you; I thought you'd be sensible about it—good-night.'

Biggles hung up the receiver and pushed the instrument away from him. Then he glanced up and saw Stella's eyes on him; for the moment he had forgotten she was there.

'Well,' she asked quietly, 'what is it?'

'Oh, nothing very much,' returned Biggles lightly.

'Your expression hardly bears out your words.'

'Even so, that is no reason why you should adopt the role of inquisitor, is it?' retorted Biggles rather coldly, as he got up from the desk.

Stella took a step forward and laid her hand on his arm. 'Won't you tell me what is happening?' she asked wistfully. 'I know you're worried. I knew it before the telephone message came. Isn't it something to do with your friend, Mr. Lacey?'

'Possibly.'

'Where is he?'

Biggles thought swiftly for a moment and then looked her straight in the eyes. 'He's a prisoner in the hands of the enemy,' he answered quietly.

Stella caught her breath. 'I see,' she said slowly. 'And what are you going to do about it?'

'Do? Nothing. There is nothing one can do, except carry on. He might be anywhere within a radius of fifteen hundred miles. If I carry on, it is quite certain that sooner or later I shall meet these thugs, and if one hair of Algy's head has been hurt—well, it'll be a bad day for them.'

'Yes, I'm quite sure it will,' she replied in a low voice. 'You'll let me know if I can do anything, won't you? You're doing so much; I'd like to think I was helping.'

'Of course,' he smiled. 'By the way, don't say anything about this to your father or Mr. Cronfelt.'

'Why not?' she asked quickly, as they walked towards the door of the hangar.

'For several reasons; one being that it might lower their confidence in Biggles & Co.'

'I understand. Good gracious!' she cried, as they reached the door. 'It's pitch dark.'

'Well, I warned you, you know.'

'Yes, you did. Still, it doesn't matter. May I leave my machine here? I'll collect it in the morning.'

'Certainly. I'd run you home in my car, but to be quite truthful, I've a lot of things to attend to, and—'

'Yes?'

'I'd rather not leave the hangar. I know I have Ginger and Smyth to look after things, but at this stage anything might happen.'

'Of course. Stay, by all means. I can get home quite easily; there are frequent coaches passing the gate.'

Biggles walked with her as far as the airport entrance, saw her safely in a public motor-coach, and then returned quickly to the hangar, where he called Ginger and Smyth into the office.

'They've got Algy,' he said bitterly.

'I was afraid of it,' muttered Ginger. 'But it's something to know he's alive. I was dreading to hear he had crashed.'

'Wait a minute, that's not all.' In a few words Biggles told them of the ultimatum that had been delivered over the telephone.

Ginger's eyes glinted as he finished. 'That's one under the belt, and no mistake,' he declared wrathfully. 'What are you going to do?'

'Wait and see if this diamond shipment that they

talk about actually comes off. So far, we've only their word for it. It's a pretty nice thing, I must say, when these crooks are able to prophesy our movements. They know more about Cronfelt & Carstairs business deals than we do.'

'Yes, it's a bit steep,' agreed Ginger. 'But suppose the diamond deal comes off, what then?'

'I shall go to Aix, and I shall hand the stones over,' replied Biggles simply. 'They may be worth fifty thousand pounds, but what's that to Algy's life?'

'Nothing! Absolutely nix,' declared Ginger emphatically.

'You see—' began Biggles, but broke off as the telephone rang again. 'This is Cronfelt, I expect,' he said without interest, as he reached for the instrument. 'Hello! Ah, good evening, Mr. Cronfelt; I was just going to call you. Yes, we had a little trouble on the way; I'll tell you about it some time . . . what's that? . . . No, the gold is quite all right. It's in the bank; I'll bring you the receipt in the morning. Lucky? . . . yes, very lucky indeed. What's that?'

Ginger, who was watching him closely, saw the muscles of his jaw tighten suddenly. 'Well?' he asked, as Biggles hung up the receiver. 'What did he say?'

Biggles took out a cigarette and tapped it mechanically on the case. 'He says he's got a valuable parcel of diamonds for shipment to Amsterdam—to-morrow,' he replied quietly.

'And you'll take them—to Aix-la-Chapelle?'

Biggles nodded.

'Am I coming with you?'

Biggles glanced up. 'No,' he said firmly. 'Definitely and finally, you are not. I'm making this trip solo.'

Chapter 5
What happened to Algy

When Algy took off from the beach in his Bulldog to follow the touring-car that had left its tracks plainly on the sand, it did not occur to him that the chase would be a long one.

Zooming up to two thousand feet, he saw the car almost at once; it was just turning away from the sea into the narrow street of a small fishing-village that nestled in the low chalk cliffs. He did not turn, or give any other indication that might have led the occupants of the car to think that he was in any way connected with the big machine they had left standing on the beach, but went straight on for a considerable distance, keeping a watchful eye, however, on the car.

He saw it mount a low hill, turn sharply to the left, and reach the main road which, at that point, ran along the brow of the cliff. Once on the open road it accelerated to a high speed and raced away towards Calais; but shortly before it reached there it took another turn, this time to the right, and roared down a straight, poplar-lined road which, after the manner of French roads, seemed to stretch to the horizon.

Algy climbed away to the right, and from his elevated position had no difficulty in watching it. Nor had he any difficulty in keeping up with it; in fact, his difficulty lay the other way, for his slowest flying speed was considerably more than the maximum speed of the car, and he was compelled to circle from time to time in order not to leave it too far behind. The only occasion on which he lessened the distance between them was when the car approached a village, and there was a slight possibility that it might turn into a building or become confused with other cars going in the same direction.

An hour passed, and still the car did not stop, and Algy began to wonder how far it was going. At one time he thought Paris was the objective, but when the car swung away from the main Paris road on an easterly course, he knew that he had been mistaken. He racked his brains to recall any big town that lay in the new direction, but he could think of none.

Another hour passed, and still the car sped on, and he began to get seriously concerned, although he congratulated himself on his foresight in having an extra petrol-tank installed against just such an emergency.

When the car did finally stop he was so taken by surprise that he overshot it by two or three miles; but the event relieved the boredom, and as he turned back towards it he watched with renewed interest. He saw that it had stopped near the gate of a large field; two of the men had got out and were walking quickly towards the corner, and following their line of march, he stared in astonishment at what he saw. He blinked and looked again, but there could be no mistake. An aeroplane was taxi-ing towards the gate from the shade of a group of trees in a corner of the field.

This put a new complexion on affairs, one for which he was quite unprepared. Yet, he reasoned, as he watched the bullion-boxes being transferred to the machine, it was not so strange after all. The only things that worried him now were whether he would have sufficient speed to keep up with the other aeroplane, and if his petrol would last out until it reached its destination. But Biggles had told him to hang on, and hang on he would, even if it meant a forced landing with empty tanks.

No great penetration was demanded to see what was going to happen. The fact that the bullion-boxes were now being loaded in the machine could only mean that the final destination of the metal was some considerable distance away. One or more of the men in the car would accompany it, leaving the driver of the car to take his vehicle to its usual garage, which might in the end turn out to be nothing more than a public parking-place in a not far distant town. Obviously he could not follow both the car and the aeroplane; not that it really mattered, for the little ingot-boxes were the crux of the situation, and sooner or later they would be certain to find their way to the headquarters of the organization.

What followed was precisely as he expected. One man got into the driver's seat of the car and drove quickly away, while the others climbed into the aeroplane, which immediately took off and swung round on a direct easterly course.

The chase was now far more to Algy's liking, particularly when he found that he could keep up with his quarry, although he was still possessed with the fear that he might run out of petrol before the game came to earth.

An hour passed, during which time the monoplane did not deviate from its course by a yard; nor did it lose height, or by any other manoeuvre indicate that it was nearing its objective. Algy had long since abandoned any pretence of trying to keep track of his position on the map. The landscape was purely agricultural, broken occasionally by forests that presently became too numerous to be identified. Small towns and villages, railway lines and long straight roads passed below in quick succession, but as landmarks they failed to help him, so he kept his eyes on the leading machine, thankful that there were no clouds to make observation difficult.

He knew that his main tank must now be very low, so he was not surprised when, a few minutes later, the engine coughed, coughed again, and, with a final splutter, expired. Instantly he switched over to the gravity tank, which contained the last few gallons of petrol he had, and which would last him not more than a quarter of an hour at the very outside.

He began to count the minutes now, noting with increasing uneasiness that the country below was becoming more broken; most of it was still under cultivation, however, and devoted almost entirely to the culture of the vine. He was actually conjecturing whether it would be possible to land, re-fuel, and afterwards find the other aeroplane on the ground by continuing on the same line of flight, when, to his infinite relief, he saw its nose dip down into a glide that could only mean that it was about to land. At that precise moment his engine cut out dead.

From his altitude of two thousand feet he had very little time to make up his mind where he was going to land; nor had he much choice in the matter of a landing-place. He saw a small village in the near distance, backed by a fir-clad hill surmounted by an imposing castle, but it was surrounded by vineyards which would have spelt disaster had he attempted to land amongst them. There was only one place in which he thought he might be able to get down, and he glided towards it, at the same time noting that the other machine had disappeared behind a belt of trees.

The field he had selected was really more of a glade between two woods than an open pasture; it was long and narrow, but fortunately ran in the right direction to the wind. What was equally important, it was level, and appeared to have a good surface. And so it proved. He 'S'-turned towards the end of the glade, side-slipped gently to bring the machine in line with the middle of it, and then ran in to a faultless dead-stick* landing.

Once on the ground he wasted no time in idle speculation. The first thing he must do, he decided, was to find out in what part of France he was. Secondly, he would have to go to the village and try to get in touch with Biggles by telephone. Thirdly—and this he feared would present more difficulty—he would have to have some petrol in his dry tanks, at least enough to take him to the nearest aerodrome; and lastly, he must try to locate his quarry. This course of action settled in his mind, and the need for urgency being apparent, he set about the fulfilment of items one and two with the greatest possible speed. Leaving the machine just where it had finished its run—for of course, he had no means of moving it—he discarded his flying-kit, tossed it into the cockpit, and set off at a brisk pace in the direction of the village.

The sun was hot, so he kept in the shade of the trees, at the same time keeping a watchful eye open for a peasant, from whom he hoped to learn something of the locality. But the countryside seemed strangely deserted. Once he saw two men in green uniforms, with guns across their knees, sitting on an eminence, and assumed

---

* Flying term for a landing when the propeller has ceased to revolve.

they were gamekeepers; but they were some distance away on the far side of a brook that he did not feel inclined to wade, so, paying no further attention to them, he hurried on in the direction of the village.

To his annoyance, for he deplored the loss of time, it took him nearly an hour to reach it; and when finally he strode, dusty and perspiring, into its one straggling street, he breathed a sigh of relief as his eyes ran over the sun-scorched windows of an irregular line of mediocre shops. But the sigh became a gasp, and he pulled up suddenly, as instinctively he read the names over the windows. Hymann . . . Schmidt . . . Wilhelmmayer . . .

'Good heavens!' he breathed, with a sudden pang of apprehension. 'I'm in Germany!'

Rather shaken by the discovery, he stood for a moment looking round, and trying to adjust his ideas to this unforeseen development. It struck him that the place was oddly quiet. A hush, almost sinister in its intensity, hung over the place, and endowed it with an atmosphere of cold hostility which, in spite of the shimmering heat, sent a little chill running down his spine. The only sign of life that he could see was a gaunt black cat that lay on a doorstep and watched him broodingly with baleful yellow eyes.

It occurred to him that the people of the village might be working in the vineyards, or possibly resting during the heat of the day, so, shaking off the unpleasant feeling of apprehension that had gripped him, he set off down the street in search of the post-office. Once or twice he thought he saw faces in the darkened rooms, eyes peering through the slats of the closed wooden shutters; and the eerie sensation of knowing he was being watched did nothing to improve his composure.

'What a perishing lot of swine they must be,' he muttered to himself, half angrily; and then slowed down as two men in green uniforms, with rifles over their arms, stepped out of a side turning. They did not speak, but there was something about their manner of approach that warned him that his fears had not been groundless. Instinctively he glanced over his shoulder for a line of retreat, and saw with surprise, but still without real alarm, that two more armed men had closed in stealthily behind him.

'Well, at least I shall be able to find out where I am,' he thought, as he waited for them to come up.

He was turning over his few words of German in his mind when they reached him, but before he could speak one of them addressed him in a harsh, arrogant voice.

Algy shook his head. 'Nix. No comprenez,' he said, feeling that he was making a fool of himself.

'*Engländer*—ha?'

'Yes—*oui*—er—*ja*. English—*ja*,' nodded Algy vigorously.

The man said something quickly to one of the others, and what was evidently a consultation took place, although Algy could not understand a word of it.

'You haff bassbort—*ja*?' demanded the first speaker, in a manner so aggressive that Algy longed to hit him.

'*Nein. Nein* passport. I've lost it —*perdu—tombé** — you know,' he replied, accompanying his remark with what was intended to be a demonstration of how his passport had fallen out of his pocket.

Any humour that there may have been in this linguis-

* French: lost—fallen

tic pantomime was lost on the other. 'How you get here?' he asked suspiciously.

Algy felt that he was on dangerous ground, and he thought swiftly. He knew that the other aeroplane could not be far away, and knew that his interrogators must be aware of it. Did they know that he, too, had arrived by air? In any case, he reasoned, there was no point in attempting to conceal it, for in order to get away he would need petrol, and as soon as he asked for it the truth would be out. He decided, therefore, that it was better to stick to the truth.

'I came by air—*par avion** . . . *flug*—in a *doppel decker***, he explained, throwing out his arms, presumably to represent planes, and giving a fairly good imitation of an aero engine.

The German nodded sombrely. 'Come,' he said shortly, and led the way down the street.

For a few minutes the strange procession filed down the road, and then the leader halted outside a small, isolated stone building. He took out a key, unlocked the door, and invited Algy to enter.

Almost unthinkingly, Algy stepped across the threshold, but leapt round with a bitter imprecation as the door slammed. For a moment he stared at it uncomprehendingly; then his eyes sped to the barred window and he understood.

'Confound it! The fools have clapped me in jail,' he snarled. Then, raising his voice, 'Hi!' he yelled, beating on the door with his fists as he heard the footsteps retreating. There was no reply, and grinding his teeth with rage and mortification, he sat down on the only

* French: by aeroplane
** German: fly . . . (in a) biplane

piece of furniture the cell contained—a wooden bed without covering of any sort—to think the matter over.

For a long time he sat and stared at the door, still unable to grasp the full significance of his detention. Curiously enough, it did not enter his head that it had any bearing on the work in which he was engaged. He thought he was simply a victim of red tape and bungling rural officiousness.

An hour passed, and his annoyance gave way to bitter indignation. He kicked the door and shouted, but these efforts produced no results. The window was high up in the wall, but by propping the bed under it he was able to climb up and see out. The view revealed nothing more interesting than a small paddock in which a cow was placidly chewing the cud, so he dropped down to the floor again at a loss to know what to do next.

For a long time, while the sun sank and the white light of day faded slowly to the purple of evening, he employed himself by composing a letter which he would insist that the Royal Aero Club should send to the German Government when he got back, protesting, in sometimes violent and sometimes plaintive language, against the treatment that had been meted out to him as a stranger in a foreign land.

From this unprofitable pursuit he was aroused sharply by the grinding of motor-car brakes outside the prison. Footsteps approached. A key grated in the lock and the door swung slowly open. Three men stood in the doorway. Two of them, who carried rifles, were in the green uniforms that were rapidly becoming familiar, so he paid no attention to them, but riveted his gaze on the other, who, standing slightly in front, was obviously an officer of superior rank.

He saw a tall, lithe, clean-cut military figure whose sunburnt face bespoke years of service in hot climates. A monocle gleamed in his right eye and accentuated the sardonic smile that played about his thin, clean-shaven lips.

How long Algy stared he never knew. His brown eyes met the cold blue ones of his *vis-à-vis* unflinchingly, and for some seconds without recognition. Then, slowly, like the earth seen through a dispersing cloud on a summer morning, his memory rolled back the mists of time, and the unbelievable truth was revealed. Suddenly, *he knew.* And the knowledge struck him like a blow.

'Good heavens!' he breathed, through lips that had turned dry. 'It's von Stalhein.'

The other nodded affably. 'Yes,' he said quietly. 'No less. And here, after all these years, is the Honourable Algernon Lacey – still scouting for trouble.'

Algy ignored the thrust. 'But I thought you were dead*,' he blurted, with an astonishment he made no attempt to conceal.

'I hoped you would,' answered von Stalhein simply. 'But we of the German Secret Service do not die so easily. It has been said that, like the cat, we have nine lives. The occasion you no doubt have in mind, when I was shot down and crashed following the ingenious coup planned by our mutual friend Bigglesworth, was my eighth life. I had one left. I still have it.'

'Then make the most of it, for you won't have it long,' Algy advised him grimly. 'You try keeping me here, and Biggles will be after you like a starving tiger.'

Von Stalhein laughed unpleasantly, and his manner

* See 'Biggles Flies East' also published by Red Fox in this series.

became reminiscent. 'Funny how the wheel of fortune turns, isn't it?' he observed. 'It's a long step from the deserts of Palestine to the verdant plains of—er—Central Europe. Do you remember___'

'Never mind about the past; I'm more interested in the present,' interrupted Algy. 'What's the idea of keeping me shut up here, anyway?'

The German shook his head sadly. 'Why be so precipitate?' he complained. 'Do you know, I believe that I should have recognized you as a disciple of Bigglesworth even if I had never seen you before. Ah, well, I forgive you. By the way, you'll be pleased to hear that I'm taking care of your machine. It seemed a pity to leave it out in the open—'

'Then perhaps you'll let me have some petrol and hand it back,' growled Algy.

The mocking humour in the German's eyes faded, but his manner remained courteous. 'Suppose we go up to the castle and discuss it?' he said suavely.

Algy did not move.

The two guards shifted their rifles on their arms, slightly; the threat was not to be ignored.

Algy drew a deep breath. 'Yes, I think it would be a good idea,' he said calmly.

'I thought you would,' replied von Stalhein softly.

Chapter 6
Ginger Gets a Shock

Ginger was taken aback by Biggles' firm refusal to allow him to take part in the flight to Aix-la-Chapelle, but he knew better than to question his chief's decision. That Biggles was in no mood to discuss, much less argue the matter, was apparent, and his frame of mind revealed more clearly than anything else could have done that he regarded the trip as the most dangerous mission he had yet undertaken.

With Algy already gone, and Biggles preparing to step into what might prove to be nothing less than a trap, it is not to be wondered at that Ginger was worried. He felt that things were moving rapidly towards a climax that would leave him in the unenviable position of having to make important decisions on his own initiative. Not that he was afraid for himself. That was an aspect that did not enter into his calculations. It was the thought of being left to act alone, when possibly he might make a bad blunder with fatal results to the desperate business in which they were engaged, that caused him to have a sleepless night and sent him early to Biggles' room with a cup of tea as an excuse, in the hope of hearing that he had changed his plans. But in this he was doomed to disappointment.

'Help Smyth to get the Cormorant ready,' Biggles told him briskly, as he dressed. 'I shall have to slip along to the office to get these diamonds, after which

I shall get off as soon as I can. You'll stand by with Smyth for any telephone messages.'

'Don't you think it would be a good thing—' began Ginger nervously, but Biggles cut him short.

'If you're going to suggest that you come on this show, then the answer is "No, I don't",' was the terse reply; and it may have been the disappointment written plainly on Ginger's face that caused Biggles to add quickly, 'I know you mean well, laddie, and all that sort of thing—but it's no use dissembling. There's serious work afoot. If the thing is a trap, it's no use both of us getting into it. You'll do more good by keeping out of the party, because then there will at least be one left who will know what has happened and be able to carry on. If I don't come back—er—that is, if you don't hear from me in a day or two, I want you to take the letter that you'll find in the top drawer of my desk to Colonel Raymond, at Scotland Yard. Don't forget.'

'I won't,' Ginger promised miserably.

'That's all, then. I'm moving off to Lombard Street now. Stand fast until I come back.'

'O.K., Chief.'

For a long time after Biggles had gone Ginger sat on a chock with his chin in his hands, considering the situation; and the more he thought of it the less he liked it. He helped Smyth to wheel the Cormorant, which had now been repaired, out on to the tarmac, and then returned to his uncomfortable seat. He caught sight of Stella's Falcon, standing well back in the hangar, and a speculative look dawned in his eyes. He walked across and examined it with renewed interest, and presently, satisfied with the inspection, he returned to the Cormorant where Smyth was standing after running up the engines.

'Smyth, what time did Miss Carstairs say she was coming down for her machine?' he asked.

'I don't know—why?'

'Don't you think it would be a good thing if we filled the tanks for her?'

Smyth started and looked round suspiciously. 'What's the idea?' he muttered. 'You be careful what you're doing. If you go and bust that machine there'll be a nice old row.'

'Who's talking about busting it?' inquired Ginger innocently.

'All right; we might as well fill her up as do nothing while we're waiting,' agreed the old flight-sergeant.

In a quarter of an hour the job was done, and Ginger stood back with a grunt of satisfaction just as the Bentley drew up and Biggles walked into the hangar.

'Everything all right?' he asked sharply.

'All on the top line, Chief,' replied Ginger. 'Got the sparklers?'

Biggles smiled, and took a small, flat, sealed package from his pocket. 'Look at that,' he said. 'Fifty thousand jimmy-o'-goblins' worth. If that little packet belonged to us, we should be able to retire on pension.'

'Well, what's the matter with hitting the breeze with it?' suggested Ginger brightly. 'We've got an aeroplane—what more do we want?'

Biggles looked shocked. 'Are you suggesting that we do a bunk with the diamonds?' he asked horrified.

'Sure! We'd have to find Algy, of course—'

'That's just what I'm going to do,' declared Biggles. 'All right, serious now. Engines running all right, Smyth?'

'Both correct, sir.'

'Good; then I'll be getting along. I expect I shall be back before nightfall, but there is a chance that I may be delayed until to-morrow. You know what to do, both of you,' added Biggles, as he climbed into the cockpit of the Cormorant.

'We do,' declared Ginger, with a curious smile.

Biggles waved his hand; the chocks were pulled away and the big machine swept across the aerodrome.

Ginger darted inside the hangar to the Falcon. 'Come on, Smyth, give me a hand,' he yelled.

'Here, what are you going to do?' asked the mechanic in a startled voice.

'I'm going to keep an eye on him, what do you think?' snapped Ginger, as they wheeled the machine out. 'Do you suppose that I'm going to sit here and twiddle my thumbs until we hear that he's been bumped off by that gang of uncivilized thugs? Not on your life. Give me a swing.'

The mechanic ran round to the propeller, but staggered back very red in the face as Stella Carstairs walked round the corner.

'What are you doing with my machine?' she asked in surprise.

'I'm just going to make sure that she's all right,' explained Ginger promptly.

'But she was perfectly all right yesterday,' protested Stella.

'Yes, I know, but the mice might have got into her during the night,' declared Ginger. 'This place is infested with vermin,' he added, as an afterthought.

'Good gracious! What—'

Ginger caught Smyth's eye. 'Contact,' he called crisply.

The engine started, and the machine began to move forward.

'If I don't come back, deliver the letter that you'll

find in the top drawer of the skipper's desk,' Ginger yelled over his shoulder to Smyth.

'How long are you going to be?' shouted Stella.

'Not long,' answered Ginger non-committally, as he opened the throttle.

Not once did he look back as he climbed steeply over the aerodrome boundary and then turned his nose eastward. Instead, he busied himself with taking out an envelope and pinning it to the instrument-board; on it were pencilled some figures denoting a quickly plotted compass course to Aix-la-Chapelle. This done, he studied the sky ahead long and carefully, but, as he expected, the Cormorant was already out of sight. This did not dismay him in the least, however, for he knew that even if Biggles flew on full throttle, the Falcon would arrive at the rendezvous within a few minutes of the larger machine.

He had several anxious moments during the flight. Once he thought that the wind had shifted, causing him to drift southward, but the smoke from a factory chimney told him that he was mistaken. Several times he studied the ground for the landmarks that, according to the maps, were due to appear, but in vain, and this also caused him some uneasiness. Not once during the trip did he catch sight of the machine in front of him, although the sky was clear, from which he assumed that Biggles was making full use of the power in his two engines.

With a slightly favourable wind he reached Aix—or the town that he hoped was Aix—in just under two hours, and at once turned south, eyes questing the ground for the rendezvous. He found it much more easily than he expected, but as he looked down his face slowly turned deathly pale.

In a large rectangular field were two aeroplanes. One, a dark green monoplane, was in the act of taking off. The other, unmistakably the Cormorant, was standing in the centre; from it arose a wisp of smoke which, even as he watched, grew swiftly in volume. A tongue of flame leapt upwards from the cabin.

Never during his wildest moments had he imagined a descent so swift and desperate as the one he now made. Not even Biggles' landing in the smoking machine on the French foreshore a few days previously could compare with it. Throttling back, he flung the Falcon into a vertical side-slip, holding the joystick right over against the side of the cockpit with both hands. With a screaming wail, the machine dropped earthward like a stone, and as it fell Ginger's eyes raced over the landscape, seeking the figure he hoped to see, but in vain.

His landing was a hair-raising thing to watch, although he did not realize it, for he took risks that normally would have appalled him; and when finally the Falcon's wheels touched the ground, only a desperate last-minute swerve prevented it from piling itself up on the now flaming Cormorant.

He was out of the cockpit before the machine had finished its run, tearing like a madman towards the blazing aeroplane, but at a distance of thirty yards he knew he was helpless to do anything. Never before had he seen an aeroplane in flames, and the awful spectacle almost overcame him. The roar of the flames and the crackle of woodwork were almost deafening, while the heat was indescribable. Even at thirty yards he could smell his clothes scorching, and feel the skin blistering on his face. Impotent, he could only stagger back with his arms uselessly trying to fight off the searing heat, and nearly driven to madness by the certain knowledge that any one who had been in the machine must already be dead. No living creature could survive in such an inferno for more than two or three seconds.

Suddenly he stopped dead, staring in unbelievable horror at the cockpit. At first he thought it was an optical illusion, a trick played upon his distraught mind by the dancing flames; but as he stared again, regardless of singeing hair and eyebrows, he knew that he was not mistaken. The pilot was still in his seat, slumped forward over the controls, with his left arm hanging down outside the cockpit.

For a few seconds Ginger went quite mad. As the full horror of the thing struck him, he screamed, and then commenced to run round the flaming wreck jabbering to himself, not knowing in the least what he was doing or what he was saying. Then suddenly he was quite calm. A fierce anger swept over him, a burning hatred such as he could never have imagined, a fury that made him tremble like a leaf, and sent him, ice-cold, towards the still purring Falcon. One thing mattered now, one thing only: revenge. The word rang in his ears like a bell as he climbed into the cockpit and pushed the throttle open savagely.

Ashen-faced, he held the joystick forward until collision with the trees on the far side of the aerodrome seemed inevitable; then he jerked it back into his stomach. The Falcon zoomed into the air like a rocket. At the top of the zoom he levelled out and glared ahead through the swirling arc of his propeller. Almost at once his eyes found what they sought; found it and held it. Far away an infinitesimal speck showed against the blue. It was the green monoplane, heading eastward.

Chapter 7
What Happened at Aix

I

When Biggles set out on his trip to Aix, with the sealed package that Cronfelt had given him in his pocket, he did not underestimate the risks he was running. Indeed, he was well aware that he was about to embark upon what was likely to prove the most desperate adventure of his career, and one that might easily be his last. Of the unscrupulous nature of the men against whom he had pitted his brains he had already had ample proof, although even yet he had not plumbed the full depth of their callous brutality.

That they would willingly release Algy in return for the gems he did not for one moment believe, but he had no other means of getting in touch with either captors or captive, so while he had accepted their terms he was prepared for any developments. He was also prepared to go to any lengths to win the round, which might, or might not, be the end of the whole undertaking.

He did not dwell upon the awkward situation that would inevitably arise if, in saving his partner, he lost the gems, particularly when it was discovered that he had made no attempt to reach Amsterdam, his avowed destination. That, he decided, was a problem to be solved if it arose. The immediate present supplied him with all the mental exercise he needed.

He kept a sharp look-out during the journey, not that he expected anything to happen, and in this his reasoning was correct, for he reached Aix without incident and without seeing another machine of any sort. With the famous continental health-resort under his left wing, he turned sharply to the right, which brought the machine on a southerly course, and forthwith began scrutinizing the country-side for the appointed rendezvous.

He was not long in finding it, and he smiled curiously when he saw a green monoplane, with its propeller ticking over, almost in the centre of the field. To say that he was not surprised when he realized that his unknown correspondent was also using an aeroplane would be incorrect. He observed the machine with genuine astonishment, because he had taken it for granted that he would be met by a motor-car, although once having perceived the aircraft he was amazed that he had not foreseen such an obvious contingency.

He noted that the machine bore no markings of any sort, but he lost no time in contemplation of this breach of international regulations. If they wished to hide the nationality of their machine, people who had proved that they were prepared to commit murder were hardly likely to let a little matter like international regulations stand in their way, he reflected, as he circled the field and then glided in to land.

Even before his wheels touched he saw three men run out of the cabin of the green machine, which, now that he was nearer, he saw was of a type unknown to him. They stood beside the wing with their faces turned upward, and calmly awaited the biplane's arrival. Nor did they move when it landed.

Biggles did not attempt any subterfuge, which, in

the circumstances, would have been a waste of time. He taxied to within a few yards of the other machine, regarded the three men stonily for a moment or two, and then, leaving his engine ticking over, he jumped down and walked towards them.

'Do we speak English?' he inquired coldly; and then raised his eyebrows as he recognized the German with the American accent who had been spokesman when he had been forced to land in northern France. The other faces, including that of the pilot, were new to him, and he wondered vaguely why the same pilot had not been employed as on the previous occasion.

The German—for there was no doubt of his nationality in spite of his American accent—eyed him malignantly. 'Yes, we shall get on faster,' he retorted, with a hostility that he made no attempt to disguise. 'You're a smart guy, aren't you,' he added evilly, obviously referring to their previous encounter.

'Let's not waste time paying each other compliments,' answered Biggles shortly. 'I want my partner; you want—what I've got in my pocket. That, I understand, is the transaction for which this meeting has been convened. Am I right?'

'Sure you are,' replied the other quickly. 'Well, pass over the stones.'

'Not so fast. What about your part of the deal? Where is my partner? If, as I assume, he is in the cabin, trot him out.' So saying, Biggles felt in his pocket and took out the sealed package.

'How do I know the stones are in that?' asked the German belligerently.

'Do you think I'm a lunatic?' snapped Biggles. 'I didn't imagine that you'd make the transfer without seeing the diamonds, or I'd have prepared a dummy.

I give you my word that this is the packet of diamonds precisely as it was handed to me this morning by the head of my firm. A glance will assure you that the seals are unbroken.'

The other held out his hand. 'Let me look,' he said.

Biggles sensed a growing tension in the air, and he watched the three men collectively for the first hostile move that he felt was coming. He was prepared for it. 'No,' he said slowly. 'Where is Lacey? Produce him, and the jewels are yours; but no partner, no jewels.'

The German laughed suddenly. 'Are you telling me?' he asked with a chuckle.

'Yes, I'm telling you,' returned Biggles, with every nerve quivering.

The German's hand went to his pocket, but by the time he had withdrawn it Biggles was covering him with an automatic. 'Careful,' he said warningly. 'Two can play at that game.'

The other put on a look of hurt surprise, and withdrew his hand, in which was a silver case. From it, he selected a cigarette with care. 'Well, now, look at that,' he said. 'And all I wanted was a smoke.' Suddenly his eyes narrowed and his voice changed. 'You looking for trouble?' he asked harshly.

'Just as you like,' returned Biggles, feeling that the talk had gone on long enough.

'All right, then, you can have it,' snarled the German. 'Take a look behind you.'

But Biggles was not to be caught by this age-old trick. 'No,' he said quietly. 'I can see all I want in front of me.'

'Maybe, but take a look all the same,' sneered a voice behind him.

Then Biggles knew, with a swift surge of anger, that

it was no bluff. Some one was in the machine. Casually he turned and looked. Projecting through the cabin window, at a distance of not more than three yards, was the most diabolical weapon ever conceived by human ingenuity — a sawn-off double-barrelled shot-gun. He did not need telling that if fired at such a range it would blow a hole straight through him the size of a tea-plate. A bullet-wound will heal in time, but a charge of small shot, fired at point-blank range, never.

'So it's like that, eh?' he said bitterly, putting his automatic back in his pocket. 'I might have known you'd put over a dirty deal,' he added viciously.

'Let us not waste time paying each other compliments,' mimicked the first speaker. 'Step inside; the boss wants a word with you.'

'Lacey isn't here, then?' asked Biggles, deeply disappointed, for although he was prepared for something on the lines of what had happened, he had hoped that Algy would be brought to the spot.

'We've plenty of weight to carry without him,' grinned the other mysteriously. 'Take a look inside and you'll see what happens to people who annoy the boss,' he invited.

Wonderingly, Biggles obeyed, but as he reached the cabin door and looked inside, he stopped short with a feeling that an icy hand was clutching his heart, for stretched along the floor was the body of a man in flying-kit. He was stone dead, and had been for some time; there was no doubt of that. Biggles recognized him at once. It was the pilot of the single-seater who had forced him to land a few days previously.

'What's the idea of this beastliness?' he asked icily.

'Watch, and you'll see,' the German told him. 'You're about to witness the last journey of the redoubtable flying Ace, Major Bigglesworth.' To this remark he added something swiftly to the others which Biggles did not catch, but they evidently understood.

As in a horrid nightmare, Biggles, still covered by the shot-gun, stood and watched the gruesome drama enacted. The body was placed in the pilot's seat of the Cormorant. A handful of tow was thrown into the cabin. A lighted match followed. A wisp of smoke curled upwards.

He needed no explanation of the reason for the ghastly outrage. The Germans had a body to dispose of, and were killing two birds with one stone, so to speak. When the remains of the body were found it would naturally be assumed that it was he who had perished, so his disappearance would cause no comment. Evil though he knew the perpetrators of this frightful deed to be from what Cronfelt had told him during their first interview, this far surpassed in horror anything he had imagined them capable of, and as he watched the smoke curling upwards he made a mental vow that he would not rest until he had brought them to justice.

'That's all; let's go. Inside, everybody,' snapped the German.

Biggles was pushed unceremoniously into the cabin. The others followed. The man with the shot-gun, who, it now transpired, was the pilot, handed the weapon over to one of the others and took his place at the controls. The engine roared. The machine swung round into the wind, bumped for a moment over the turf, and then soared into the air.

Biggles had flown many aeroplanes in many lands, but the flight that now commenced provided a new sensation. For once he was flying as a passenger, with the control of the machine in the hands of a man whom he did not know. Moreover, he was on a flight of unknown duration to a problematical destination. He did not even know the name of the country to which he was flying, or, for that matter, over which he was flying, for without a compass to guide him he could only gather a very broad idea of direction from the angle of the sun's rays across the cabin. Seated as he was between two of his captors, he could only just see out of the cabin windows, and from this position he was, of course, unable to look down, so the only part of the landscape visible was the distant horizon.

In these unpleasant circumstances the time passed slowly, and he began to long for the break in the regular drone of the engine that would foretell the end of the journey. An hour went by, but still there was no indication that they were nearing their objective, and he resumed his cogitations wearily.

The jewel-box had been taken from him at the beginning of the flight, and he wondered vaguely how Cronfelt and the others would feel when they heard of their loss. But the thing uppermost in his mind was the knowledge that he might soon have an opportunity of speaking to Algy, and possibly learning from him something of the men to whom they were opposed.

The monotonous purr of the engine was finally lulling him to sleep when it died away suddenly and the nose of the machine dipped downward. He was alert instantly, for it seemed that at last the end of the journey was at hand. Nor was he mistaken, and he leaned forward eagerly in the hope of catching a glimpse of the ground, only to be thrust back roughly by one of the men who sat beside him. Worse was still to come, for before the machine touched the ground a bandage had been bound over his eyes, so that when the machine ran to a standstill he was even worse off than he had been in the air, for he could see nothing at all. Naturally, he protested against this indignity, but in the face of the shot-gun argument was futile, and he submitted with the best grace he could muster.

In what followed he was guided entirely by sound and touch. He was led for some distance across yielding turf, although whether it was a regular aerodrome or a private field he had no means of knowing. Then his feet crunched for a few minutes on hard gravel, after which he was assisted into a motor-car. To his relief, the ride was of short duration, and a few minutes later, after climbing a steep gradient, the car stopped and he once more stood on a hard road. There was a sharp military word of command that might have been uttered by a sentry on duty; a door opened and the gravel under his feet was replaced by a firm stone floor. Unseen hands guided him along a corridor.

'Pick up your feet – there are steps in front of you,' said the voice of the German. He felt with his foot for the first one, found it, and another.

The staircase became a nightmare; it seemed to go on for ever, and one hundred and eighty winding steps he counted before he was told to stop. It struck him as odd that he should be taken upwards, for according to tradition prisoners were invariably led down to their cells.

The hands that had guided him were removed, and

somewhere close at hand a heavy door slammed. Some moments he stood still, awaiting the next instructions, but as they did not come he lifted an arm tentatively. Somewhat to his surprise the silence remained unbroken, and with a queer feeling of expectancy he whipped the bandage from his eyes. For a second he stood blinking like an owl in the light, staring about him stupidly, for the scene was not in the least what he had expected to see.

He found himself in a small circular room of cold grey stone, furnished with bare necessities as a bedroom, and lighted by a single window, about thirty inches square, and some four feet from the ground, through which the afternoon sun flung a shaft of white light on the massive oaken door. The furniture, which comprised a squat bed and oddly-shaped chair, was of the same material, and on both the same device, a seven-headed eagle, was carved in medieval style. The room and its equipment was obviously of great age, and, if proof of this were needed, it was supplied by the thickness of the walls, revealed by the cavity in which the window was sunk. Originally the opening had evidently been unglazed, but now a thin beading of varnished wood held a single sheet of glass in place.

So much Biggles saw at a glance as he turned his head slowly to survey his prison, and the brief inspection answered the question that was now of paramount importance. The only means of egress, except the door, was the window, and to this he now turned his attention.

Again a single glance told him all he needed to know, and he pursed his lips as he looked through the rather dirty pane of glass, for while the scene was unquestionably impressive, from his point of view it was distinctly depressing.

He saw that the room in which he was confined was situated in a turret of one of those magnificent yet forbidding castles that still raise their grey, weather-worn battlements above the sombre, ever-green forests of the Rhineland, to bear silent witness of an age of knights in armour, of dragons, and damsels in distress. It was built on a slight knoll, the lower flanks of which were clad in close-growing fir-trees whose drooping boughs cast a sable shadow over the hill-side as if in mourning for the days that were no more. In the distance they gave way to open fields and vineyards, where peasants were at work gathering the grapes in great baskets which, from time to time, were emptied into ox-carts of antiquated pattern.

The actual structure was composed of huge blocks of hand-hewn stone that rose tier upon tier for nearly a hundred feet, although the vast area of the place dispelled any impression of disproportionate height. At one end, crenellated walls ended in imposing corner turrets whose feet were planted in what had once been a moat, but was now a large pool of stagnant water with steeply sloping banks from which sprang a riot of ferns that reflected their images in the black water without giving any clue to its depth. The water ended about half-way along the side of the main building, as if an attempt had been made at some time to fill in the moat, so that the walls at the opposite end dropped into dry ground that was broken at intervals by groups of gnarled, sun-starved shrubs.

From the pile of debris which emerged from the water at the foot of the wall at the turreted end, a tangle of ivy, as old as the castle itself, flung groping, octopus-like arms upwards to the very top, and formed a nesting-place for a colony of ravens whose heads protruded, gargoyle-fashion, from the complicated mesh of branches. That was all Biggles could see from his limited viewpoint, but it was sufficient to show that the window, as a means of escape, was utterly out of the question. There was not a cornice, a crevice, nor even a fingerhold within reach. Above was the sky; below, the moat. Between them was a perpendicular wall of stone, worn smooth by the winds and rains of ages. Admittedly, the top of the ivy-covered wall came to within some fifteen feet of his turret window, but it was below and to the right, and there was no possible means of reaching it.

'Well, I needn't waste any more time looking for a way out on this side,' he brooded, as he gazed out over the landscape now bathed in the soft glow of evening. 'What I should like to know is if Algy is here,' he mused, as he turned back into the room. His eyes fell on the bed-coverings, and he examined them with a view to employing them as a rope, but they consisted only of a threadbare blanket and two flimsy sheets that would not have supported the weight of a child, and he threw them where they belonged impatiently.

There was no need to examine the walls, for they were of solid stone, broken only by the window and the door.

'Well, there's only one way out of this place and that's through the door,' was his unspoken thought, as he sat down in the chair and waited for the next move in the game that now looked like ending in drama.

He had not long to wait. After a peremptory knock, the door was pushed open and a menial, carrying a cloth-covered tray, entered. Behind him were two men in the inevitable green uniform, each with a revolver in his hand.

Biggles looked at the weapons and then at the men's faces. 'You're not taking any chances, I see,' he sneered, hoping to induce them to say something. But the ruse failed. The tray was set down on the bed and the party withdrew without a word.

Biggles removed the cloth. 'Well, they're not going to starve me to death, evidently,' he thought, as his eyes fell on a pot of tea, bread and butter, jam, and several slices of home-made cake.

Half an hour later, when the servant returned with the same escort as before to remove the tray, both the tea-pot and the plates were empty, and Biggles was leaning in the window recess with his elbows resting on the broad stone ledge, gazing across the peaceful country-side in the same posture, no doubt, as many a prisoner before him had adopted. Like theirs, his thoughts ran in one channel, that of escape, and he did not even turn as the men went out again. The heavy door swung to with a dull boom; a key grated in the lock, and he was once more alone.

Chapter 8
Out of the Frying-Pan

For a long time, while the evening glow faded slowly to purple twilight, he stared with unseeing eyes across the drooping firs to the now deserted vineyards beyond, wrestling with the problems presented by the situation that had arisen, and to which there appeared to be no immediate answer. He concluded that he could only wait and snatch at any opportunity to escape that might occur.

The air was sultry, as if a thunderstorm was impending, and the atmosphere of the little cell grew unbearably stuffy. There was no hinge or hasp on the window, so there was no means of opening it, but the remedy was obvious. Unhurriedly he returned to the bed, wrapped a portion of the blanket round his fist, and went back to the window. A single punch, and the shattered glass tinkled musically as it struck against the stone wall on its long fall into the moat. The remaining jagged edges removed, he threw the blanket aside and resumed his original position, breathing the fresh air with relief and satisfaction.

By leaning out beyond the area previously checked by the glass, he found that he could now command a slightly better view of the ground immediately below, but it appeared to hold nothing of interest, and he was about to turn away when a movement at the edge of the firs attracted his attention. Feeling that any distraction, however trivial, was better than none, he looked again, and saw that he had not been mistaken. A dark figure was moving furtively through the trees, dodging from one to the other with the silent stealth of an Indian on the warpath, and pausing from time to time to listen. The face, glowing oddly white in the gloom, appeared to be turned upwards as if attracted by the noise of the breaking glass.

As Biggles watched this intriguing behaviour an extraordinary sensation crept over him. It came so slowly that he could not tell when or how it began, but it increased in intensity, and his casual glance became an unbelieving stare. Moreover, it affected him so strangely that his hands trembled and his lips turned dry For he thought he was looking at Ginger. Indeed, his eyes told him so, but his brain refused to accept this apparent demonstration of a miracle. Running counter to his increasing conviction that it *was* Ginger, was a line of common-sense thought that told him that it was impossible. How could Ginger have reached the spot in such a short time, even if he had known where it was? How could he have found his way to the walls of a castle of which he had certainly never heard, and which was nothing more than a pin-point in the remote heart of Europe? A queer sense of unreality stole over him, and he shook his head impatiently as the thought struck him that his nerves were playing him tricks. The figure had stopped now, clear of the trees, and was gazing upward, eyes scanning the grey walls. It was Ginger—or it was Ginger's ghost. Biggles was not sure which. Hitherto he had firmly refused to accept the existence of such things as spirits, but he began to suspect that he had been wrong.

At that moment Ginger saw him. Biggles knew that he had seen him by the way he started and stared and then raised his hand in a curious gesture that he had acquired, after much practice, from his favourite gangster film hero.

Biggles was no longer in doubt, and he had opened his lips to call out when something made him take a swift glance to left and right to make sure that no one was in sight. And it was a good thing that he did so, for there, not a stone's throw away, was one of the green-uniformed guards, rifle on arm, and an enormous mastiff at his heels. What was worse, the man was walking along the lip of the moat in the direction of the very spot on which Ginger stood, apparently making an evening patrol of the castle walls.

Biggles' heart turned cold, for he thought that Ginger would call out to him before he could prevent it, in which case his discovery would be swift and certain, for in the hush that preceded nightfall the man could not fail to hear a twig snap, much less the sound of a human voice.

Biggles acted with a speed that surprised even himself, for he could see that Ginger, from his position, would not see the guard until he was within a yard or two of him. To shout a warning was out of the question. To wave a signal which the guard, who was now looking up at him, would also have seen would have been equally fatal. What he did was not original, but it was effective, and it may have been the only solution to the problem. He opened his lips and sang, loudly, as if he was anxious for the whole world to hear. The tune was the first one that came into his mind, and it was well chosen, for it was the British National Anthem. To the tune of 'God Save the King' he chanted such words of warning as poured into his head, although, almost as if he were inspired, they fell easily into the tune:

114

'Look out, there is a Hun,
Quite near you with a gun,
    He has a dog;
He is com-ing your way,
He'll see you if you stay,
I'll let you know when it's O.K.—
    Do-n't make a noise.'

As Biggles' first words shattered the evening silence
several things happened at once, and they were all so
ludicrous that he could hardly sing for laughing.

Ginger staggered back and threw up his arms as if
he had been struck a physical blow. Recovering, he
stared upwards with a dreadful expression on his face
that said more plainly than words that he thought his
chief had gone raving mad. Simultaneously, a score of
ravens burst from the ivy with loud croaks of alarm;
the mastiff threw up its head and gave vent to a long
melancholy howl; a waterhen that had been floating
placidly on the moat disappeared as if it had been
drawn under by an anchor, leaving only a bubble and
an ever-widening ring to mark the spot where it had
been; and the guard jerked up his rifle and crouched
as if he expected to be attacked at any moment.

As the last words of the extempore song died away
Ginger, after a swift wave to show that he had understood, faded into the shadows behind him. The guard
increased his pace, looking upwards at the tiny window,
and for one awful moment Biggles thought that he had
understood the words. But it was soon clear that he
had not done so, and Biggles hailed him cheerily.

'Good evening, Major. Any sport?' he called.

The man scowled but made no reply, and it was
obvious that he had not understood. Satisfied that this

was so, Biggles placed his thumb to his nose and extended his fingers in the time-honoured manner to signify his contempt in a way that could not be misinterpreted. Further, he hoped by this means to draw the fellow into a conversation that might yield information, but in this he was unsuccessful. The man looked away and presently disappeared round the corner of the building.

But Biggles was taking no chances. He gave him a good ten minutes to make sure that he was well clear, and then made his second vocal contribution to music, employing the same tune as before:

> 'The Hun is out of sight,
> Round the wing on your right,
>   Keep your eyes skinned.
> I hav-en't got a hope
> Unless I get a rope;
> You'd better go and do a slope
>   To-o Lon-don Town.'

As an afterthought he added:
'Hip-hip, tell *Ray*-mond. . . . hip-hip, tell *Ray*mond.'

As the last words echoed to silence he strained his eyes in the deepening gloom for a signal from Ginger to show that he had heard; but none came. Minutes passed, and still by neither sign nor sound did Ginger reveal his presence. That he would come back Biggles felt quite certain, and he settled himself down to wait with a new hope in his heart.

The time passed slowly. The rim of the sun disappeared behind a range of distant hills, and darkness fell. Presently a narrow crescent moon arose and flooded the scene with its wan light, but below the window all was enshrouded in profound darkness.

The only sound that broke the silence was the soft lapping of the water on the edge of the moat as a rat or otter pursued its nocturnal way. Looking down, Biggles could see the moonbeams dancing on the ripples. A few minutes later he started, as, with a loud cry and a swish of leaves, a bird burst from the ivy and flapped away into the night. Another followed, and Biggles caught his breath sharply. From somewhere not far away came the sound of laboured breathing.

'That you, Ginger?' he said softly.

'O.K., Chief, I'm coming,' was the whispered reply.

'For God's sake take care you don't fall,' breathed Biggles, as in something like a panic he understood the perilous climb in which Ginger was engaged. But he said no more, knowing that no good purpose could be served. If Ginger was climbing the ivy, presumably in order to get on to the roof of the main building, nothing he could say could help him, so he remained silent, although more than once he clenched his hands as a louder swish than usual frightened him into the belief that Ginger had slipped.

'All right; I'm on top,' came Ginger's voice presently. 'I can just see your head against the sky.'

'And I can just see you,' replied Biggles quickly, as he made out a dark form astride the crenellated wall.

'How far are we apart, do you think?' asked Ginger.

'About five yards.'

'Then we shall just be able to do it,' came Ginger's voice confidently. 'Stand by to catch the rope.'

Biggles stiffened. 'Rope! Have you got a rope?' he gasped.

'Yes.'

'What's the idea?'

'If I can get the end to you, you can pull it in, tie it to something inside your room, and then shin down it.'

'You're sure it's long enough?'

'I think so.'

'Think! You only think! Great Scott! I don't want to be stuck half-way.'

'It was the best I could do; it should just reach to the water.'

'How deep is the water?'

'I don't know, but I couldn't touch bottom as I swam across.'

'How are you going to get down?'

'The same way as I got up—by the ivy. I'll meet you at the bottom.'

'The rope isn't likely to break, is it?'

'I don't think so. It isn't rope, it's leather. I got all the reins out of the harness-room and buckled them together.'

Biggles felt a sinking sensation in the pit of his stomach. 'But are you sure they'll hold?' he persisted.

'I hope so.'

'So do I,' muttered Biggles fervently, deciding to leave congratulations on Ginger's brilliant piece of work until he was safely on *terra firma*. 'All right, let's have it,' he whispered.

The rope swished through the air. He missed it the first time, and had to wait until Ginger had coiled it for another throw. Again he missed, but the third time it fell on his arm, and he grabbed the end just as it was sliding off.

'Good,' called Ginger. 'Don't pull, or you'll have me off. The rest of it is wound round me. Take it gently while I pay it out.'

Biggles got back into the room and drew the leather

118

reins in slowly, checking them with his fingers for weak places as he did so. This done, he looked about him for the best means of securing the end before he lowered the remainder into the moat, but in the act of doing so he heard a sound that brought his heart into his mouth. Footsteps were coming along the corridor outside.

There was just time to kick the leather coils under the bed when a light gleamed below the door and the oak swung inwards to admit the same three men as on the last occasion. As before, the servant carried a tray, and one of the guards held up a small oil lamp which, after he was in the room, he set down on the floor.

The other guard noticed the broken window at once, and said something quietly to his companion, who looked at it, and then at Biggles, with an expression that showed that he had no fear that the prisoner would depart that way.

Biggles' heart was thumping wildly; so much so, in fact, that he was afraid his jailers would notice his anxiety, for he was terrified that Ginger, not understanding the silence, would speak.

But Ginger evidently guessed what was happening, for he made no sound; as a matter of detail, he afterwards told Biggles that he saw the glow of the lamp reflected on the edge of the window recess, and knew that some one had brought a light into the room. Listening, he heard the door shut, but did not see Biggles sink down on the bed and wipe away the perspiration that had broken out on his forehead under the strain.

He was up again at once, however, anxious to proceed with his ordeal, and rather alarmed in case the guards came back. He thought it was fairly certain that they would return for the tray after about the same interval of time as before, and he considered the possibility of leaving his exit until after they had gone; but on second thoughts he abandoned the idea, particularly in view of the possibility of a surprise visit from the man whom his captors had referred to as 'the Boss'.

'No,' he decided. 'The sooner I am down the better'; and suiting the action to the thought, he pulled the reins from under the bed, which he dragged across to the window. This done, he fastened one end securely, and lowered the other slowly through the window. That it did not reach the water was certain, for there was neither sound nor ripple, but how far it fell short he was unable to see. Ginger, he observed, was still perched on the crenellated wall.

'I've just had visitors,' he told him, as he lowered himself through the window.

'So I thought,' was the reply. 'Are you going down now?'

'Yes; I'll see you at the bottom,' replied Biggles, with an assurance he was far from feeling, as he gripped the reins and swung clear. He had a ghastly moment as the bed moved a trifle and he thought his knot was slipping, but it steadied itself and he began to lower himself hand over hand.

Before he was half-way down he knew his strength would not hold out until he reached the bottom, for the reins were too thin for him to get any grip with his knees, and the heavy dew that was falling had made them greasy. Slowly but surely they began to slip through his wildly gripping fingers. He knew that if once he started to slip in earnest nothing could check his fall, and the buckles which he encountered at intervals were likely to tear the palms from his hands. He derived some comfort from the knowledge that every fresh grip he took brought him nearer to the bottom, and was just congratulating himself that the worst was over when his dangling legs told him that he had reached the end of the line.

Desperately he was trying to look down to see how far he had to fall, when the line started slipping through his fingers, and before he could take a fresh grip he had slipped off the end. For one horrible instant he held his breath, and then, with a terrific splash, he was in the moat. The shock of the sudden immersion was greater than that of the actual impact, and almost before the water had closed over his head he was striking out. But something seemed to be clutching at his legs, subtly yet firmly, and he knew he was in the grip of the long ribbon-like weeds that curled upwards from the ooze at the bottom.

Forgetting all the oft-repeated advice he had heard about allowing one's legs to hang limply in such circumstances, he kicked out in a blind panic, and reached the surface with a mighty gasp. With a stroke that was something between a dog's paddle and a crawl, he managed to reach the bank just as Ginger, shedding water at every step, came running along.

'My goodness, what a shocking noise you made!' he muttered apprehensively, as he held out his hand and hauled Biggles up the wall. 'The people inside will think that a walrus has drifted in.'

'They can think I'm a school of whales if they like,' snarled Biggles, unwinding coils of slimy weed from his neck and body. 'I'm nothing for this Jack Sheppard* business; it's too unnerving. Besides, I'm wet through.'

'I'm not surprised,' observed Ginger. 'As a matter

---

* English highwayman 1704–24, renowned for his repeated escapes from prison.

of fact, I'm a trifle damp myself,' he added, taking off his coat and wringing it out. 'The water seems particularly wet to-night, doesn't it?'

'And your ear will be particularly thick if you try to be funny,' growled Biggles. 'Thank goodness it isn't cold,' he went on, rising to his feet and shaking himself like a dog. 'Hark!'

For some seconds they stood quite still, listening, but there were no sounds to suggest that Biggles' noisy exodus had been observed or heard.

'Come on,' said Ginger quietly. 'I know the way.'

'Where to?'

'The machine.'

'What machine?'

'Miss Carstairs'.'

'Great goodness! Have you stolen her Falcon?'

'No, I've only borrowed it.'

'She *will* be pleased.'

'She ought to be, too, when she knows what I've borrowed it for,' replied Ginger meaningly. 'But come on; I can't stand any more shocks. When I looked up and saw your face at the window I thought I was seeing a ghost. I could have sworn I saw some one in the Cormorant when she was burning.'

'You did—but it wasn't me,' returned Biggles grimly. 'I'll tell you about that later, though. Have you seen anything of Algy?'

'Great Scott, no! Why, is he here?'

'I expect so. We can't go without him, or at any rate without making sure that he isn't here. Moreover, these skunks have got the diamonds. I shall have to get them back, too.'

'What are you thinking of doing—going to the front door and asking for them?'

'No, I'm going to help myself,' replied Biggles promptly.

Ginger stared aghast. 'Do you mean that you're going back inside that place after I've just got you out?'

Biggles nodded. 'It's the safest place around here for miles,' he declared. 'My escape will probably be discovered within half an hour, and then there'll be a rare old hue and cry. The last place they'll think of looking for me is inside the *Schloss*.'

'In the what?'

'The *Schloss*—castle.'

'Good name. Well, go ahead; I should have thought you'd have had all the sloshing you want for one night.'

'I have, but I've got to find Algy. Let's start this way.'

'I've been along there.'

'What is there?'

'Empty stables, harness-room, out-buildings, and a little power-station—looks like electric-light plant. There's another turret on the castle like the one at this end.'

'Then let's go and look at it.'

They soon reached the buildings Ginger had described. There were rows of empty stables, bespeaking former glories, and several out-buildings, in one of which a small power-plant was running.

'Yes, it's the electric-light plant; direct current by the look of it,' observed Biggles quietly after a peep through the window. 'There's nobody in there, either. I tell you what. If I manage to get into the castle, and get into a jam, I'll whistle. If I do, run in here and switch all the lights off. It might give me a chance if the whole place was plunged into darkness.'

Ginger grinned. 'I'll remember that,' he said.

Biggles turned and faced the formidable mass of the

castle itself. As Ginger had said, there was a turret exactly like the one in which he had been confined at the opposite end. From the small square window a yellow light glowed feebly. 'If he's here, that's where he is for a certainty,' he said tersely.

'There's no ivy at this end, though, and nothing but a fly could get up that wall,' muttered Ginger ruefully.

'I'm afraid you're right. The only way to get to that room is from the inside,' replied Biggles quietly. 'I wonder what's going on in there,' he added, pointing to a row of tall, church-like windows on the first floor, obviously in the wall of the same room, and from which a warm yellow light streamed out and cut oblique shafts through the outer darkness. Several of them were open.

'Not much use guessing,' suggested Ginger.

'That's what I was thinking. Let's hunt round and find a ladder; there's bound to be a ladder in a place like this.'

He was quite right: there was. They found half a dozen, of various lengths, slung on giant hooks at the back of the stables.

Ginger regarded them doubtfully. 'Are you seriously contemplating hauling one of these across the courtyard and shoving it up against one of those windows?' he asked anxiously.

'I am. What did you think I was going to do with it—make myself a pair of stilts?'

'It seems a crazy business to me,' ventured Ginger.

'It probably is,' agreed Biggles. 'But not being a bird, I can't look into that room without something to stand on.'

'It's asking for trouble.'

'Lay hold, and don't talk so much,' Biggles told him. It was the work of only a few moments to unhook

one of the ladders and carry it across the cobbled courtyard to one of the lighted windows, the sill of which
was about fourteen or fifteen feet above the level of the
ground. Biggles paused for a moment to listen, but all
was silent, so he ran quietly up the rungs of the ladder
and peeped over the edge of the sill.

Ginger saw him stare; heard his quick intake of
breath; watched him throw a leg over the sill and
disappear from sight. With bated breath he awaited
his return. The seconds ticked by, but he did not
reappear. The seconds grew into minutes, and still he
did not come. Then, just as he was about to risk a peep
into the mysterious chamber, he heard something that
sent him nearly frantic with alarm. It was the sound
of measured footsteps quickly approaching.

He knew that he must do something, and do it
quickly, and his first thought was of the ladder, the
suspicious position of which could not fail to be noticed
and would certainly be the signal for an alarm when
the new-comer reached the spot. Biggles, he decided,
would either have to remain in the room or drop to the
ground; but the ladder must come down. Bracing his
muscles, he dragged it sideways, exerting every ounce
of strength he possessed to prevent it falling with a
crash into the sparse shrubbery that formed the garden
border beneath the windows.

To a great extent he was successful, but at the loss
of his own equilibrium. The ladder struck the bushes
with a dull *swoosh*, and he measured his length beside it.

The footsteps were almost upon him now, and to
move would have been fatal; so, hardly daring to
breathe, with his face in his arms and his body pressed
as close as possible to the warm earth, he lay still and
waited.

Chapter 9
Into the fire

I

When Biggles looked over the window-sill into the room he had not the remotest idea of what he expected to see. At the back of his mind he had a vague hope of seeing some of the members of the gang, possibly the leader whom the others called the Boss, and had he been successful in this he would have reckoned the risk he was taking well worth while. But to his intense astonishment the room was empty. He looked swiftly to left and right to make quite sure this was the case, and then, after an all-embracing glance around the vast chamber, his eyes automatically turned to the most outstanding piece of furniture in the room, which was a ponderous carved table in the centre. Around it a number of chairs were arranged, with a very large one at the head, as if for a committee meeting. This impression was strengthened by the fact that a blotting-pad, bound in red leather, with a large silver ink-stand in front of it, occupied a prominent place on the table in front of the large chair.

On the blotting-pad lay the object that made Biggles catch his breath. It was the sealed package that had been given to him by the Cronfelt that very morning. And the seals were still unbroken. This was an amazing stroke of luck that he certainly did not expect, and he lost no time in taking advantage of it. He swung his legs over the sill and darted towards the table.

His object was quite clear in his mind. He intended pocketing the package and returning to the window in the shortest possible space of time. But while he was still half-way across the room he heard a slight noise, and in one breathless glance saw the door slowly opening. To reach the window again without being seen was obviously out of the question, yet to reach the package before the new-comer crossed the threshold was equally impossible. And there was no time to think. The only possible hiding-place that he could see at that moment was the clear space behind the door, which was nearer to him than the table, so without pausing in his stride, he altered his course and darted towards it.

The plan was a forlorn hope at the best, and like most forlorn hopes it failed. It is true that Biggles reached his objective, but it was preposterous to suppose that his swift rush across the room had not been heard. It had. The door was slammed shut, and he found himself staring into the astonished eyes of a flunkey dressed in medieval style.

Now Biggles had the advantage of surprise. The flunkey did not know what he was going to see, but broadly speaking Biggles did, and he utilized the opportunity offered by that knowledge. Before the man could move or speak, or even before he had thought of doing either of these things, Biggles' clenched fist shot out like a piston in a vicious upper-cut, which made contact with that vulnerable spot known in boxing circles as the solar plexus. The recipient of this unpleasant salutation uttered a spasmodic gasp; a spasm of agony convulsed his face, and he collapsed like a pricked balloon on to the floor.

Biggles looked at the door. It was shut. Then he committed what, a minute later, he knew was an error

127

of judgement. But then it was too late to rectify it. He knew that what he should have done was to have left the man where he had fallen, grabbed the jewel-box, and bolted. But for some reason which he could never understand, his first thought in that vital moment was that he must conceal the insensible victim of his attack. The impulse to do so was so strong that he thought of nothing else, although in the background of his mind he was anxious to seize the box and be gone. However that may be, the fact remains that he seized the fallen man by the collar, and snatching up the wig that had dropped from his head with the other hand, commenced to drag him towards a small door that stood ajar a few yards farther down the room. Reaching it, he dropped his limp burden inside, and had taken the first step towards the table when he heard voices near at hand. The door through which his victim had come again swung open, and he knew that he had left the package until too late. He just had time to step back into the doorway behind him when several people walked into the room he had just vacated.

Mentally kicking himself for bungling things so badly, he turned to seek a way of escape, but to his horrified surprise he saw that he was in nothing more than an alcove from which there was no other exit. There was not even a window. The shock of this discovery brought beads of perspiration to his face, for he saw in an instant how desperate was his position. To reach the door or the window through which he had entered, without being seen by the men in the room, was out of the question; yet to remain where he was, was to invite disaster, for in a few minutes at the outside the man on the floor would recover consciousness, whereupon it was only to be expected that he would lose no time in making his predicament known to every one within earshot. In fiction he could, of course, have been bound and gagged, and Biggles was prepared to inflict both these indignities on him. Indeed, he would have been delighted to have done so, for it would at once have solved the problem. Unfortunately there was nothing with which to do the binding and gagging. Far from finding any rope, there was not, as far as he could see, an inch of string available. There was not so much as a picture on the wall from which he might have removed the cord, and groping in his pocket for his handkerchief with a wild idea of using it as a gag, he found that he had even lost that.

For a moment it seemed that all was lost, and he was contemplating a wild dash to the window, when he got an inspiration. The man on the floor was about his own build. If he could get into his plum-coloured velvet jacket and knee breeches, and put on the wig, which would help the disguise, there was just a chance that he might be able to reach the door unremarked by the men now sitting round the table. Could he do it? He decided to try.

It took him nearly ten minutes to effect the change, and the fact that towards the end of that time the man on the floor showed signs of returning consciousness did not make the task any easier. So it was with fingers that trembled slightly from the ordeal of suspense, for he expected to hear his victim call out at any moment, that he finally buttoned up the purple jacket and adjusted the wig on his head. Then, without any loss of time, he peered through the crack of the door.

Along the sides of the table, some nine or ten feet distant, four men were seated, looking towards one who sat in the speaker's chair and addressed them earnestly, while he held the jewel-box in one hand and a small penknife in the other. His back was partly towards Biggles, so he could not see his face. Two of the others had their backs directly towards him. The faces of the others he could see, and a glance showed that they were strangers to him.

The room itself was more of a museum than a living-room. At one time it had evidently been the banqueting-hall of the castle, for a minstrels' gallery ran the entire length of one end; below it was a small door that appeared to give access to it. The black timbers of the roof that met overhead sloped down to the walls and met others, between which were life-sized portraits of men in the clothes of bygone days. At intervals were the tall, diamond-paned windows, surmounted by intricate Gothic tracery and flanked by rich, rose-coloured, brocade curtains that once must have been gorgeous but were now sadly faded and, in places, shredded by the ravages of generations of moths. Spanning the room from side to side were three enormous beams whose rugged sides had never known a saw or plane; from these were suspended three multiple-lighted chandeliers, with electric-light bulbs in place of the candles for which they had originally been designed.

All these things Biggles saw in much less time than they take to describe, and while he hesitated to take the plunge a low moan behind him supplied the necessary incentive. Another minute and it would be too late, so he pushed the door open boldly and walked out into the room.

The two men who were facing him glanced up as he reached the end of the table, but looked back again at once to the speaker, who was still talking in a low voice, and it was obvious that they did not consider his appearance worthy of comment. The success of the plan seemed assured, for another half a dozen paces would have seen Biggles at the door; but at that precise moment an unlooked-for incident occurred. The man at the head of the table concluded his speech abruptly, at the same time cutting the twine that was wound round the package. With a deft movement he slipped off the outer covering, exposing a red morocco case. There was a sharp snap as he slipped the catch, threw it open, and exposed the interior. As he made the last movement he started speaking again, but his voice suddenly died away and a deathly hush settled on the room. The box was empty.

Biggles, who had been watching the scene out of the corner of his eye as he passed, stopped dead, staring at the case incredulously, for once shaken completely off his guard. He forgot where he was and what he was doing. He forgot everything except the one inexplicable, unbelievable fact that the case was empty. For perhaps three seconds he remained thus, and then, as if actuated by an irresistible magnet, he felt his gaze drawn to the leader's eyes. As it came to rest upon him he felt the blood drain from his face as his entire system reacted violently to such a shock as he had never before experienced. It was not the round muzzle of the automatic that appeared over the edge of the table that caused it; it was the shock of recognition. For the face into which he was staring was that of a man who, he thought, was buried deep in the arid sand of Palestine. It was Erich von Stalhein, once second in command of German Intelligence in the Middle East.

It was von Stalhein who broke the silence. 'Major Bigglesworth,' he said quietly, 'years ago I reported to my Higher Command that you had more nerve than

131

any other officer in the British Flying Corps—no, don't move, please.'

At the sound of the well-remembered voice Biggles' nerves slipped back to normal like a piece of elastic when it is released from tension. He bowed. 'And I, Hauptmann von Stalhein, once had the honour to make the same report concerning you to the Commander-in-Chief of the British Expeditionary Force in Palestine,' he replied gravely.

A ghost of a smile flitted across the face of the German. 'Thank you,' he said. 'But allow me,' he continued quickly. 'Gentlemen, permit me to present Major Bigglesworth, D.S.O., late of the Royal Flying Corps, and now Managing Director of the civil airline operating under the title of Biggles & Company. He paused, and eyed Biggles quizzically. 'Your new uniform fits badly, if I may say so,' he observed critically.

Biggles smiled faintly. 'I haven't had time to see my tailor about it yet,' he confessed, apologetically.

'Why bother? You won't need it any longer, will you,' von Stalhein told him quickly. 'Where did you leave your clothes?'

'In the alcove.'

'Better put them on again; we shall then be able to discuss the situation with the dignity it demands,' suggested the German.

Biggles nodded. 'Perhaps it would be as well,'he admitted, returning to the alcove, where he changed quickly into his hastily discarded suit.

'Tell me, Bigglesworth,' continued von Stalhein in a hurt voice when he returned to the room, 'why did you bring me an empty box?'

Biggles shrugged his shoulders. 'Say, rather, why

should I bring you an empty box, considering what was at stake?'

'Are you inferring that you did not know it was empty?'

'I am not inferring; I am telling you.'

'Would you swear to that?'

'No, but I give my word. In fact, I would have been prepared to stake my life that the diamonds were in that case. Indeed, when you examine the situation closely, you will perceive that I may, in fact, have done just that.'

'I am glad you have not overlooked the contingency,' replied von Stalhein drily. 'Really, Bigglesworth, I hate to doubt your word, but —'

'What do you suppose I came into this room for?' interrupted Biggles. 'To waste my time and risk my life trying to recover an empty box? Be sensible, my dear fellow.'

Von Stalhein nodded slowly. 'Yes, I believe you,' he said. 'But can you think of any reason why you should be asked to take an empty box to Amsterdam?'

'I can.'

'Why?'

'Because the sender did not want the jewels to fall into your hands, obviously.'

A curious gleam came into the German's cold eyes. 'Ah,' he breathed. 'Of course. Right well you say obviously.'

Biggles felt that there was more behind the sentence than the mere words implied, but he said nothing.

'Bigglesworth,' continued von Stalhein softly, 'you must realize that you have placed yourself in a very serious position. As I suspect you were well aware at the time, if I had been in command at Zabala, years ago, instead of being under the thumb of that imbecile, von Faubourg, things would have fallen out very differently. But here I am in supreme command; this time there will be no mistake about your disposal.'

'Don't blame von Faubourg,' put in Biggles imperturbably. 'No command is proof against the unexpected, and no commander knows all that is happening inside his own headquarters.'

Von Stalhein wrinkled his forehead. 'In what way do you mean?'

'May I give you an illustration?'

'By all means; it would be interesting.'

'Then watch,' smiled Biggles. He placed two fingers in his mouth, and blew; a shrill whistle pealed through the room.

'Well?' asked von Stalhein, with a curious expression, as Biggles lowered his hand. 'Nothing appears to have happened.'

'But it will,' Biggles assured him.

At that moment all the lights went out.

Simultaneously Biggles dropped on to his hands and knees; a fraction of a second later von Stalhein's weapon blazed. It was a close call, and Biggles felt the bullet brush his hair as he dropped. He did not make for the door which, he imagined, was what the German would expect. And it was as well that he did not do so, for twice von Stalhein fired in that direction, blindly, it is true, but at such a range he could hardly have missed any one attempting to go out. Each time he fired a streak of orange flame leapt across the room, and showed Biggles what he was trying to find, which was the small door leading into what he imagined to be the minstrels' gallery.

Von Stalhein was snarling like an angry dog, and one

of the others was yelling at the top of his voice. Biggles caught the word *kerze** as he felt for the latch, and with a gasp of relief pushed the door open and locked it on the other side. His greatest fear had been that he would find it locked, with the key on the wrong side.

It was, of course, pitch dark, and instinctively he felt for his pocket to find some matches, only to remember with a growl of disappointment that he had left them in his jacket pocket. Not that they would have been any use after their immersion in the moat, he consoled himself by thinking.

'My goodness,' he muttered, as he put out his hand and groped for the wall, 'I should never be able to find my way about this place *with* a light, much less without one.'

He had already dismissed the astounding revelation of the empty jewel-case from his mind, and his one concern now was to find Algy. If only he could do that he would have been more than willing to shake the dust of the ancient building from his feet for ever. He had every confidence that Ginger would be able to take care of himself, and with this comforting reflection he tried to visualize his present position in relation to the eastern turret in which he suspected that Algy was confined. But, as he had already observed, progress without a light was likely to be painfully slow.

His groping hand encountered something long and cold, and his questioning fingers told him that it was a sword, curved like a dragoon's sabre, hanging on the wall. With some difficulty he unhooked it, and with the confidence that possession of a weapon brings, he turned to proceed, thrusting the sword out in front of him in

* German: candle

the darkness as a feeler. Quite unexpectedly the point encountered something hard, something that rang with a metallic clang, and while he was wondering what it could be, his eardrums were almost shattered by a most appalling crash. The din was so terrific, and he was so utterly unprepared for anything of the sort, that he recoiled, and collided with another object that gave way before his weight. Again there was a fearful noise as a mass of metal crashed to the stone floor, and he bit his lip to steady himself.

'My goodness,' he gasped, 'this is awful. I shall go crazy if it goes on. What the dickens am I in?'

At that instant the lights came on again and the answer to his question was plain. He saw that he was in a long corridor furnished as an armoury; or perhaps it would be more correct to say as a museum, for the weapons that were arranged in serried ranks and complicated patterns on the wall were not modern, but dated back through the ages from the nineteenth-century musket to the arquebus. Arranged on low pedestals at intervals were suits of armour; two were lying at full length on the stone-flagged floor, and there was no need to look farther for the cause of the noise that had startled him. All this he took in at one sweeping glance. In more propitious circumstances he would have liked to examine this interesting collection of military ingenuity, but the present was obviously not the time, and after a swift glance at the door behind him he hurried down the corridor, not knowing in the least where he was going, but anxious to remove himself as far and as quickly as possible from von Stalhein and his companions, who, he felt, might at this stage shoot if they caught sight of him.

Here and there he noticed glass-fronted wall-cabinets

containing powder-flasks, shot-pouches, and specimens of old-fashioned cartridges. An idea struck him, and he picked up a cylindrical round of ammunition that might have been designed for a large-bore shot-gun. Stamped on the side of it, under a film of dust, were the words 'Fabrique Nationale', and below, 'Schneider'. Ranged beside the case from which he had taken it were several rifles of antique pattern, and he had tried four of them before he found one the breech of which was designed to take the cartridge he had selected. There was no magazine, not that he had any more cartridges to fill it in any case, so he slipped the round into the breech and drove home the heavy, old-fashioned bolt. Deciding that this was a better weapon than the cutlass, he discarded his *arme blanche**, and, with the rifle at the ready, hastened to the far end of the armoury.

An open window offered an opportunity of checking his position with that part of the moat which he had already seen. To his relief, he saw that he was still on the same side of the building, and, what was even more encouraging, heading in the direction of the turret in which he had decided mentally that Algy—if indeed he was in the castle—was locked up.

He reached the far door and opened it stealthily, only to find that it led into another great room which, unlighted except for the pale rays of the moon, he was just able to see was equipped as a private chapel. There were two or three small doors in the sides, but none of them showed him what he was anxious to find, which was a flight of stairs leading upwards. He heard a whistle being blown somewhere outside, and shouts from the different parts of the grounds told him that the chase

* Cutting and thrusting weapon

was on in earnest. What Ginger was doing he dared not think; he could only trust that his ready wit and nimble feet would lead him to some place of security, although how he was ever to find him again it was beyond his imagination to conceive. The fear-inspiring baying of a hound joined in the medley of noises, and he drew a deep breath.

'Suffering Icarus, I certainly have stirred up a hornets' nest and no mistake,' he muttered, feeling his way along to the far end of the chapel in the hope of finding another exit.

He found one, but approached it without enthusiasm, for it was a small, unimportant-looking portal, narrow, with an arched lintel, and looked as if it might lead simply to a vestry or sacristy. Trying the handle, he found that it was unlocked, so, opening it gently, he peeped in. Whatever lay beyond was in darkness, but as his eyes grew accustomed to the gloom he could just make out a narrow corridor.

'Well, I might as well try it,' he thought, as he stepped inside and felt his way along the wall. A dozen paces and he was brought to a stop by another door, which a second's quiet investigation proved to be unlocked also. His nerves tightened as he opened it quietly and peeped out, and then stood blinking in a light which, although soft, was almost blinding after the darkness through which he had come.

He found himself looking out on to a spacious landing, half-way up a magnificent flight of stairs, obviously the main staircase of the castle. The balustrade was of wood, carved in a simple yet striking formal design, which every few yards carried a faded, painted shield. A crimson pile carpet covered the broad stairs to within a foot of either side, while from the walls portraits of lords and ladies in costumes of long ago gazed down with unseeing eyes upon the shrinking figure in the doorway. To the left the stairs led downwards; to the right, upwards and, he hoped, towards his objective. Not a soul was in sight, so after a moment's indecision, with the rifle at the ready, he walked boldly up the stairs. He felt that there was no point in acting otherwise, for there was nothing behind which he could hide should he encounter any one.

Twenty steps, and the stairs ended at an imposing passage that crossed the head of the staircase at right angles. Sconces projected from the walls at regular intervals, illuminating more portraits and the doors of what he took to be bedrooms. 'Heads left, tails right,' he muttered, taking a coin from his pocket. 'Tails! Right it is then.' Without further thought or ceremony, he walked quickly down the passage, looking eagerly ahead for another flight of stairs leading upwards.

He had not gone far when a sound of voices not far distant brought him to an abrupt halt, and a quick anxious look showed him that they were coming from a doorway, which he could see was open a few inches, a little farther down the passage. While he waited, uncertain how to proceed, another voice broke in upon the others. It was unmistakable, and at the sound of it he caught his breath. For it was von Stalhein's. And that he was in a cold fury was clear from the bitter, biting quality of his tone.

Now every instinct of common sense told Biggles that he ought to return the way he had come. Yet opposed to that was a curiosity that would not be denied, and drew him irresistibly towards the vertical slit of light between the door and doorpost. Just what he expected to see he did not stop to think, but what he saw, while natural enough in the circumstances, was so unexpected that he remained staring until it was a wonder he was not discovered forthwith.

The room was a beautifully appointed apartment, something between a library and an office. Superb tapestries covered the walls from the floor to the ceiling, which was painted with pictures depicting incidents from the New Testament. From the centre of it a gilded chain supported a huge unlighted chandelier bearing a thousand pieces of cut glass, the prismatic facets of which reflected, with all the colours of the spectrum, the light from the only source of illumination in the room, which was a tall reading-lamp on an imposing writing-desk.

At the desk, in a high-backed, brocade-covered chair, sat von Stalhein. He had pushed the chair back from the desk so that it was balanced on its rear legs, a position he maintained by pressing his feet against the bulbous supports of the desk. From this position he regarded no less than seven men who stood around him in various attitudes. In a rough semicircle behind him were the four men whom Biggles had seen with him in the dining-room. In front of the desk were two of the well-known green guards, with their rifles drawn into their sides in military fashion and obviously acting as escort to the prisoner who stood between them. The prisoner was Algy.

At the moment that Biggles made his surreptitious peep, which was prolonged into an astonished stare, von Stalhein was speaking over his shoulder to his four dining-room companions, while with his right hand he pointed to something that lay on the desk. Instinctively Biggles' eyes followed the pointing finger, and what he saw made them open wider than they already were.

There were two objects. The first he recognized at once. It was the jewel-case that Cronfelt had given him that morning with the wrapping-paper, still bearing the seals, beside it. The other object was a similar case. It was open, and from a bed of black velvet shimmered a number of magnificent precious stones.

Biggles had learnt a little German during his previous affair with von Stalhein; his knowledge was rusty from lack of use, but he was able to gather that the German was calling attention to the seals on both cases, presumably for purposes of comparison. That he had been engaged in this debate when Algy had been brought into the room became clear when he suddenly broke off with a shrug of his shoulders, and faced the prisoner as if he was about to subject him to an interrogation. Algy was not in the least intimidated by his surroundings, for his hands were thrust deep in his trousers pockets, and he eyed his old enemy with a faint smile which held both derision and defiance.

Biggles' first thought, when he had recovered from the mental confusion into which this unlooked-for development had thrown him, was that now, if ever, was the moment to effect a rescue. He did not think too far ahead. The first thing was to get Algy away from his guards; after that matters would have to take their course.

His eyes swept down to the door-handle, seeking the key, but to his disgust he saw that it was on the inside; he could just see the handle of it through the four or five inches of aperture provided by the opening. Glancing up again, he saw that all eyes were on the prisoner. Outwardly calm, but with every nerve fluttering like a flying wire on a bumpy day, he slipped his hand through the crack and with infinite care withdrew the key, afterwards inserting it quietly in the keyhole on the outside of the door. This done, he breathed again, for unconsciously he held his breath during a moment of such strain that the gentle scraping of his sleeve against the door had sounded like the harsh rattle of tissue paper.

For a second he waited to steady himself, and then, raising the muzzle of his rifle inch by inch, he brought the sights in line with the bulb of the reading-lamp. In the ordinary way, at such a range he would have been confident of hitting it every time, but so much was now at stake that the sights blurred and danced before his eyes. By sheer effort of will he focused them, and his fingers tightened on the trigger.

Click!

There was a metallic snap as the hammer fell uselessly. It was followed by a faint sizzling sound inside the breech.

As if controlled by a master spring, eight pairs of eyes switched round on him.

That moment will live in Biggles' memory for ever. Never in all his long and varied experience had he been so completely taken aback, so utterly shaken. The ridiculous climax, when every nerve in his body had been screwed up to breaking-point, was almost like a blow. For an instant the room rocked, and he was incapable of movement.

Von Stalhein broke the ghastly silence. As imperturbable as ever, he raised his eyebrows and a sneer curled round his lips. 'Your powder seems to be a trifle damp, Bigglesworth,' he observed dryly.

Biggles half lowered the rifle. 'Yes,' he said quietly. 'I hope you'll tell your armourer what I think about it.'

At that moment the rifle went off. With the roar of a bursting bomb rather than a small-arms cartridge, it spat a mighty cloud of smoke into the room. There was a crash of splintering glass as the soft leaden bullet ploughed its way through the chandelier and scored a long weal across the body of a cherub on the ceiling who was in the act of tossing a bouquet of flowers into the air. Coincidental with the roar of the explosion and the crash of glass, several other things happened. The recoil tore the loosely held rifle from Biggles' hands and it fell to the floor. The nearest guard ducked convulsively, as well he might, for the bullet had passed within a couple of inches of his head. Von Stalhein started, his imperturbability shattered for once, presumably under the impression that Biggles was employing *force majeure* with a vengeance. He lost his somewhat precarious balance, made a wild clutch at the nearest edge of the desk, missed it, and turned head over heels backwards into the fireplace, which, fortunately for him, was empty.

If Biggles had been shaken when the weapon misfired, he was thunderstruck when it went off. Nor could he think if a satisfactory explanation of the mystery, although he vaguely recalled having read, or being told, that in certain early types of cartridges, at the period when breech-loading guns were just coming into use, there was a definite delay between the time the cap was struck by the hammer and the resultant explosion.

While von Stalhein was still scrambling up from the fireplace into which he had fallen, Algy decided to take a hand in the proceedings. With a terrific back-handed swipe he sent the reading-lamp flying and plunged the room into complete darkness. Following this signal success where Biggles had failed, chaos reigned, but in a moment he was at the door. Biggles slammed it and locked it, and then stepped aside as it was wrenched forcibly from the inside. He moved just in time, for a bullet ripped a long splinter out of a panel and hurled it across the passage.

'Which way?' gasped Algy breathlessly.

'Any way you like; it's all the same to me,' replied Biggles, darting off down the passage with Algy at his heels. 'A window is our best chance. We've got to find Ginger; he's outside somewhere—or he was.'

II

Breathless, they reached the top of the main staircase, and were about to descend when the sound of many footsteps running up the stairs caused them to alter their plans with desperate speed.

'We shall have to keep straight on and look for another way down,' said Biggles tersely, as he doubled back and carried on down the passage. But before he had taken a dozen paces a confused murmur of voices in front caused him to halt again. At the same moment a crash and a clamour from the corridor behind them suggested that von Stalhein had succeeded in breaking open the door of his study.

'The place is buzzing like a wasps' nest,' declared Algy with commendable calmness, but darting anxious glances in all directions. 'It's time we were out of it,' he added as an afterthought.

'Funny, I was thinking the same thing,' agreed Biggles sarcastically. 'Where does this lead to, I wonder?' He indicated a narrow corridor on their right.

Algy peered in. 'There's a flight of stairs,' he said, 'but they lead upwards, not downwards, so that's no use.'

But a sudden shout close at hand reminded them that they could not be choosers, and they sped up the narrow flight of stairs anxious to see what was at the top. The staircase was a long one, and at the end of it they found their way barred by a door.

Biggles turned the handle gently; a barely audible intake of breath expressed his relief at finding it unlocked, and he peeped in cautiously. There was no light in the room, but by the wan beams of the moon they could see that they were looking into a half-furnished apartment, and a faint musty smell suggested that it was seldom used. Another door stood wide open on the opposite side.

'Well, what do we do—go on or go back?' asked Algy.

'Go on.' Biggles crossed the room, and peering through the far doorway found himself staring into a big unfurnished chamber. He was about to turn away when, as before, he saw another door on the far side. Without a word he crossed over, but when he found that there was yet another empty room beyond he turned to Algy with an exclamation of disgust. 'It looks as if we're doomed to wander about until we die of starvation,' he opined impatiently.

'Never mind, keep going; there's another door on the far side,' Algy told him. 'We shall come to something presently.'

'Probably another empty room,' returned Biggles savagely, gazing into yet another deserted chamber. Seven more they crossed, and then they came to the end, for the seventh had no door except the one by which they had entered.

'Well, that's that. Seems as if we've had our walk for nothing,' muttered Biggles grimly. 'Hark! . . . Sounds as if the Boche are on our trail, too,' he went on, as several pairs of heavy boots clattered on the distant stairs.

'Yes, they're following us all right,' agreed Algy, as the footsteps drew nearer. 'It's strange; you'd think there'd be some sort of way down—'

'Hold hard! What's this?' Biggles had taken a quick pace towards the corner of the room, and Algy, peering forward, saw what appeared to be a crude ladder fixed perpendicularly to the wall.

Biggles ran up the rungs until he was brought to a stop by a square of unpainted wood let into the ceiling at that point. Raising his hand, he pushed on it and found, as he suspected, that it was a trapdoor; it swung open easily, but his exclamation of satisfaction was drowned by the crash of the door as it fell outwards on its hinges. A draught of cool air met his face. A moment later he had pulled himself up through the opening, and was standing on the roof, with Algy, who had followed him, by his side.

Not until this moment did either of them realize fully the vast size of the castle, or appreciate how far the style of the structure had been dictated by the necessity for defence; for the flat roof, bounded on all sides by an embattled parapet, stretched far away into the darkness. At each corner a conical turret overhung the void, clinging precariously to the wall like a swallow's nest.

A few swift steps look them to the parapet. A single downward glance, and Biggles drew back hastily. 'My goodness!' he gasped. 'What a drop.'

'Yes, it seems quite a long way down,' replied Algy. 'But the point is, where do we go from here? I can hear those toughs coming along through the rooms. They can only come through the trap one at a time, so we ought to be able to hold the place indefinitely.'

'Until we starve to death, in fact,' sneered Biggles. 'No, I don't think it's much good using force at this stage. Our only chance is to try to hoodwink them by leading them to believe that we didn't come up here at all. Put the trap-door back; they'll know we're here if they find it open.'

Obediently Algy replaced the hatch, and then rejoined Biggles near the parapet.

'Come on, let's explore,' whispered Biggles, and began to creep carefully along inside the wall.

There was no need for them to go far, however, to see that they were much worse off than they expected, for not only was there no way down to the ground, but there was only one possible place of concealment. A little to one side of the middle of the roof loomed a round structure, not unlike the top of a well, and towards this they made their way.

Biggles leaned over the breast-high stonework. The reek of stale smoke struck his nostrils, and he half turned away with a gesture of despair. 'It's the chimney,' he said.

'Pretty hefty chimney,' observed Algy.

Biggles nodded. 'Collects the flues of the whole building and shoots all the smoke out here,' he said quietly. 'It's the old-fashioned idea. The modern chimney is comparatively new. Wait a minute,' he added quickly as a thought struck him. 'If I remember rightly, chimneys used to be swept by poor little devils who had to climb up and down them and brush the soot off by hand. I saw such a chimney once, in England; it had iron steps driven into the side. Have you got any matches?' Algy produced a box. Leaning over, Biggles struck a match and held it as far down as possible in the pit. 'My gosh, I'm right,' he whispered eagerly. 'Look, there's the top rung. Over you go — quickly.'

Algy hung back. 'Are you proposing to go down that

black hole of Calcutta? We shall be out of the frying-pan into the fire in every sense of the word.'

'The fires aren't alight; it's midsummer. There's no need for us to go right down. Let's go far enough to prevent us being seen by these fellows if they happen to look. I'll go first. Don't kick more soot on me than you can help.' So saying, he swung a leg over the yawning abyss, and feeling for the iron rung with his foot, disappeared from view.

Algy followed.

'All right; that's far enough,' came Biggles' voice from below. 'You stand so that you can see the trap-door; if those fellows come out on to the roof, give a touch with your foot and we'll go lower.'

'O.K.,' breathed Algy. 'S-sh. Look out! they're coming.'

Without waiting for anything more, they began to feel their way down the shaft, slowly, and not without some trepidation, for the result of a fall would, they realized, be fatal.

'All right; you'll do,' whispered Algy at last. 'We're a good twenty feet down.'

For a long time nothing happened, but then the sound of voices slowly drew near, and what seemed to be an altercation took place at the top of the shaft. Then a match flared suddenly.

Algy, knowing that it would be more than likely that his white face would be seen if he looked up, kept his head down, and bit his lips as the hot match-stalk, released by the lighter, went down his neck. Another match was struck, and a few minutes afterwards the voices slowly receded.

For what seemed an eternity, but was probably not more than half an hour, the fugitives remained in their uncomfortable positions without speaking, and then Biggles tapped Algy lightly on the ankle. 'Go and have a peep to see if they've gone,' he breathed.

Algy found it was easier going up than coming down, for he could see the vague outlines of the big iron staples against the round patch of sky, and he quickly reached the top. For the last foot he raised himself inch by inch until his eyes grew level with the rim, and as they probed the moonlight around he let out a gasp of thankfulness. 'They've gone,' he said shortly, and climbed out on to the roof, where a moment later Biggles joined him.

'I'm not sorry to be out of that,' he muttered, as he shook a cloud of soot from his clothes. 'All the same,' he went on, 'we had better stick around here for a bit in case they come back. In any case, the moon will be gone in a minute, and I'm not going to risk pitching over the parapet in the dark. It must be getting on towards daylight, anyway; the sun should be up about half-past four. Have you got the time on you? My watch has stopped.'

'So has mine,' Algy told him.

'How long have we been wandering about this dolls' house?'

'I've no idea; seems like weeks.'

'Well we can't do anything for the moment. Really, I think this is, without exception, the craziest business we were ever in. Let's sit down. There's no point in standing when one can sit.'

They made themselves as comfortable as possible against the superstructure of the chimney, squatting down and drawing up their knees, and listening for any sounds that might indicate what was going on below them.

'We've one thing to be thankful for, and that is that it isn't winter time,' remarked Algy optimistically.

'You're right there,' admitted Biggles. 'But the thing that worries me is Ginger. What will he think?'

'Don't ask me.'

'He's bound to get anxious, and as like as not he'll try to find us. I left the poor little blighter standing at the bottom of the ladder under the dining-room window; I didn't even tell him I was going in.'

'I shouldn't worry; he's well able to take care of himself.'

'Let's hope he is,' answered Biggles moodily.

The moon disappeared behind the distant forest, and Stygian darkness enveloped them. The brooding hush that always seems to mark the last hour of night settled over the landscape. Once, far away, an owl hooted mournfully, and something splashed furtively in the moat.

'I wish I knew what that kid was doing,' murmured Biggles sleepily.

But Algy did not answer. His head had slumped forward and his breathing had become the deep, regular respiration of sleep.

Chapter 10
Ginger's Night Out

It was perhaps a good thing that Biggles did not know what had become of Ginger, or he would have been a good deal more worried about him than he was. He would not have been content to rest on the roof, that is certain. The chances are that he would have gone down again into the castle. What the result of that move would have been it is, of course, impossible to say, but things would certainly have fallen out very differently from the way they did.

For Ginger the night had been even more harrowing than it had been for the others, for being alone he missed the advantage of the moral support that the presence of a comrade brings; and added to this was the burning anxiety of not knowing what fate had overtaken Biggles—a matter that worried him more than his own sufferings.

The last he had seen of his Chief was when Biggles, without any indication of what he proposed to do, had climbed from the top of the ladder into the lighted room. Immediately afterwards, the approach of one who could only be an enemy had necessitated the prompt removal of the ladder, and as he lay in the shrubbery waiting for the danger to pass, he was not so much concerned with his own predicament as to what would happen if Biggles returned to the window to find the ladder gone, and an enemy passing by. The situation was desperate, and he was nearly at his wits' end with impatience for the man to pass in order that he might put up the ladder again, when he heard a sound that put all other thoughts from his head. It was a soft pat-pat, accompanied by a sniffing sound that could only have been made by a dog.

The danger had been bad enough before, but this, he felt, was the last straw. And so it proved. The man did not even hesitate as he drew level, and actually walked some yards past the spot where Ginger lay endeavouring to quiet his palpitating heart; it is quite certain that but for the behaviour of the hound he would have gone straight on.

Ginger could sense the very moment that the hound winded him. He heard it stop; heard the sniffing cease, and knew that its muzzle was pointing in his direction, questing his exact position. It was a dreadful moment, for he knew that discovery was inevitable. Presently the hound would come forward, and, if it was the same one that he had seen earlier in the evening, he knew that he would be lucky if he escaped with nothing worse than a severe mauling. So he acted promptly, for, his attention attracted by the suspicious behaviour of the hound, the man had stopped and was now coming back.

Fortunately, Ginger had a good idea of his immediate surroundings, for he had had time to study them while Biggles was standing on the ladder, and to this he unquestionably owed his preservation, although the course he adopted would hardly have been possible for any one older than himself, and consequently less nimble.

Grabbing a handful of loose earth, he sprang to his feet and hurled it with all his force at the hound, whose position he could pretty well judge. The animal sprang back with a growl, and this provided him with the brief interval of time upon which the success of his plan hung. Above him spread an ancient rhododendron-bush, its topmost branches mingling with the broad limb of a great cedar-tree that stood some twenty paces away. Up the rhododendron Ginger went like a cat. The hound sprang, and its teeth met in the turn-up of his trousers. For a moment it was touch and go. The brute hung on with commendable determination. So did Ginger. His foot was firmly planted in a fork or he must have fallen. Even so, something had to give way, and in the end it was the cloth. The hound crashed backwards into the shrubbery, and Ginger scrambled on to the cedar with the agility of a monkey.

The man below shouted something, but he spoke in German, and Ginger had no idea of what he meant. Not that he would have paid any attention if he had. Why the fellow did not shoot was always a mystery to him, although, later on, after giving the matter some thought, he concluded that the man must have been unarmed. Possibly he was off duty, and was simply taking an evening stroll.

Anyway, with his hands torn and his hair full of cedar-needles, Ginger reached the bole of the tree where the darkness was intense. The hound had followed on the ground, and he could hear it growling deeply in its throat as it pawed the resisting wood. Looking around in desperation, he perceived that another arm of the tree stretched far over the roof of the stables, and he saw that if he crawled along it he would be able to drop to the ground with the stables between him and his pursuers. This would give him two or three minutes' start, for both man and beast would have to go round the end of the buildings in order to reach him. This seemed to present his only chance of getting away, and he set about its accomplishment forthwith.

At that moment Biggles' shrill whistle cut through the air.

Ginger literally gasped with alarm, for he had forgotten all about the signal—and Biggles, too, if the truth be admitted—and he set off with frantic haste towards his objective. His speed was his undoing. There was a sharp crack as a branch snapped. He made a wild grab at another to save himself from falling, missed it, lost his balance completely, and bumped heavily on to the stable roof. The fall was not more than a few feet, but even so it jerked the breath from his body, which did not prevent him, however, from grabbing wildly at the roof down which he was now sliding. But the tiles provided only a smooth surface, although by pressing his arms against them he was able to retard his progress somewhat. Arriving at the end of the roof, his hands clutched wildly at the guttering. They found it, and clung to it with the desperation of terror; but it was as brittle as pie-crust, and the next second he had struck the earth amid a shower of tiles and broken guttering. Luckily he had fallen on the right side of the ridge— that is, the side away from his pursuers—so he had, in fact, achieved his original object, although not in the manner he had planned.

He was on his feet in an instant, racing towards the yellow square of light that marked the window of the power-house; what with his fear of the hound, and the knowledge that Biggles must be in danger, he ran as he had never run before. Without waiting to look in the window to see if the coast was clear, he burst open the door and hurtled inside, but in the split second that elapsed between the time of his entry and the time it took him to reach the main switch, he saw that the room was no longer unoccupied. A man was in the act of pouring oil, or water, into a tank behind the engine; at least, he *had* been in the act of pouring, but with Ginger's whirlwind arrival, he dropped the can in alarm. By that time Ginger had swept his hand across the switch and plunged the place in darkness. Not complete darkness, however, for a lighted candle that the carctaker had brought with him continued to throw a wan light over the scene from the iron bracket on which it rested. From the direction of the castle, above the confused noises going on inside the power-house, came a sharp report, although he was only vaguely conscious of it; nearer at hand he could hear the baying of the hound, so he rushed back to the door, slammed it shut and bolted it.

But the other man had not been idle, and by the time Ginger had turned he was almost upon him. With something between a snarl and a sob Ginger cast about for a weapon, but there was nothing, and in the confined space there was little room to dodge; yet he did his best, and, due as much to luck as skill, he succeeded beyond his wildest hopes.

The man made a final rush, but Ginger ducked under his arm and darted towards the candle with the idea of putting it out. In order to reach it he had to pass under the long driving-belt that ran from the oil engine on one side of the room to the dynamo on the other. He had no difficulty in doing this, and sent the candle spinning with a sweep of his arm. But his pursuer was not so successful. Whether he forgot the belt altogether, or whether in the darkness he misjudged his distance, Ginger never knew, but there was a wild yell of pain

155

and fear, mingled with an unpleasant *swoosh* as he ran headlong into it. This was followed by a vicious threshing of the belt as it ran off the driving-wheel. The engine, released of its braking influence, raced to a screaming crescendo, making such an appalling noise that Ginger cowered back with his hands over his ears, fearful lest the thing should jump from its bed and flatten him against the wall.

Yet with all this he did not lose his head, although his next act was instinctive rather than the result of definite thought. What had become of the engine attendant he did not know; he could not see him, or hear him, although he could hear the original guard beating on the bolted door with his fists. There was only one other way out, and that was through the window, and towards the square of starlight that marked its position Ginger groped his way. It opened more easily than he expected. A quick vault, a wriggle, and he was through, panting on the soft earth outside. The hound, he guessed, was on the opposite side of the building with the guard, who was now trying to force open the door, but he did not wait to confirm this. Instead, he sprinted away as fast as the darkness would permit. He did not know where he was going, nor did he particularly care. He was gasping from exhaustion, and his one idea at that moment was to place himself as far as possible from the guard, the engineer, and the hound. That done, he would look for a hiding-place where he could recover his composure and work out a plan of campaign.

The thing that worried him most was the report he now remembered hearing immediately after he had switched off the light. Was it a gunshot? A pistol shot? The sharp, deep bark suggested the latter. If so, it could only mean that Biggles was involved in trouble in the castle. What ought he to do? Suppose Biggles ran to the window in dire emergency, only to find that the ladder had been removed? True, the distance to the ground was not great, so if necessary he could drop, but he might tear himself badly on the bushes, or sprain an ankle—or even a leg. Again, the very absence of the ladder might cause him to hang back suspecting a trap.

As he struggled on Ginger hardly knew what to do for the best. He was in the last stages of mental and physical exhaustion, and the only scrap of comfort he could find was in the fact that the hound had not yet picked up his trail. In the ordinary way he was naturally fond of animals, but had he possessed a weapon he would have shot the hound with the greatest of pleasure, for apart from the fact that it was evidently a vicious brute, in the darkness its nose was a far greater danger than the eyes of its master.

Breathing heavily, he turned his steps towards the stables, feeling that they would yield the best hiding-place, and presently broke cover under the cedar-tree in whose branches he had taken refuge a few minutes previously. Looking up at the window through which Biggles had disappeared, he saw with a shock that the lights were on again, from which he deduced that the guard had either managed to get into the power-station or the engineer had recovered sufficiently to resume his work. For a moment or two he stopped to listen, with his head inclined towards the engine-room, but he could hear no sounds of pursuit; nor did any sound come from the room above. Had he time to re-erect the ladder? He thought he had. At any rate, it was worth trying. Afterwards, he decided, he could climb back into the tree, from where he would be able to watch the window for Biggles with small risk of discovery, at least, until daylight.

To find the ladder was a simple matter and he dragged it out of the bushes. Staggering and swaying under its weight, he managed to get it upright, and allow the top to fall against the open window in the same position as before. Well satisfied, he was about to turn away when something—it may have been a sound, or it may have been instinct—made him glance towards the power-station. The hound, crouching low, was running at him with bared teeth.

For the fraction of a second he stood still, petrified with fear and surprise, and then he did the most natural thing in the world. Without the slightest regard for what might be at the top, he went up the ladder like a lamplighter. At the top he stopped and looked down; the hound was standing at the base with its feet on the bottom rungs, glaring upwards and snarling in its throat. Two men were running towards the spot from the power-station.

Ginger became desperate. He felt that the business was getting altogether beyond him; that he was moving in one of those nightmares which repeat themselves indefinitely without ever reaching a conclusion. He knew that he could not go on much longer, and the knowledge caused him to act with an utter disregard for consequences. He could not remain where he was, that was certain. That he could not go back was equally plain. Therefore he had to go on. From the top of the ladder he looked into the room. To his surprise it was empty, so without further hesitation and without the slightest idea of what he was going to do, he crept inside.

A backward glance showed the two men at the

bottom of the ladder; one of them was actually on it, following him. Ginger seized the top rung and tried desperately to push the ladder over, but with the man's weight on it, it was too heavy for him to move, and he turned back again to the room, realizing that he would not be able to remain in it. He must go on. But where? He saw that there were two doors, and chose the smaller one, thinking it would be less likely to be used; but before he could reach it it was flung open from the other side and two green guards appeared. They were, of course, looking for Biggles, but Ginger was not to know that.

Turning on his heel, he saw his original pursuer just climbing over the window-sill, so he made a wild rush at the other door. The strange sensation that he was doing what he had once seen in a funny film came over him, but the humour no longer made any appeal. He reached the door with the guards close behind and dashed down the corridor he discovered on the other side. He found a flight of stairs leading up to it, and down these he went at a dangerous speed, only to find that they ended in another corridor, at the end of which he found his progress barred by a green, baize-covered door. He could hear footsteps close behind, but in his panic he did not stop to employ the usual tactics of caution; he threw the door open and charged in, only to stop dead with a curious gesture of consternation and finality, for the room was full of green guards. There must have been a dozen or more of them. The room was evidently their barracks or mess-room, for their accoutrements hung from pegs on the walls. Near the fireplace stood a slim man with cold, blue eyes and a close-cropped head; he seemed to be in a towering rage, but at Ginger's abrupt entry he broke off in what he was saying and raised his eyebrows.

Ginger felt two pairs of hands seize him from behind.

The blue-eyed man nodded slowly. 'Welcome,' he said in a tone of biting sarcasm. 'Your timely arrival will save us the trouble of looking for you. As soon as it is light enough to see, I will make an example of you that should discourage your friends from pursuing their meddlesome activities.'

Ginger nodded. 'That's O.K. by me,' he said cheerfully. 'Do you mind if I sit down?'

Chapter 11
Back to the Wall

In spite of his desire to keep awake, Biggles must have dozed, for he was suddenly aware that dawn had broken, and was flooding the surrounding hills with a pale yellow glow. He nudged Algy in the ribs with his elbow. 'Come on, laddie,' he said, 'let's be moving. There seems to be something going on underneath.'

They both scrambled to their feet, walked to the parapet and looked down.

One glance, and Biggles had clutched Algy's arm in a grip of iron. A frenzied exclamation broke from his lips as he stared in horror-stricken amazement.

Eighty feet below was a walled courtyard in which a scene was being enacted that could only have one meaning. Some ten or a dozen of the green guards were standing in a row with their rifles at the 'order arms' position. Opposite them, perhaps ten yards away, stood Ginger. There was no mistaking his figure, although a bandage had been bound over his eyes. On the steps that led down into the courtyard, scowling malevolently, stood von Stalhein.

'They're not going to shoot him,' gasped Algy in a strangled voice.

'They are,' replied Biggles coldly. 'And quickly, unless we do something about it,' he added grimly. He raised himself up and leaned over the parapet. His face was grey, and his nostrils quivered; his eyes gleamed like polished steel. 'Von Stalhein,' he called sharply.

In the breathless hush of dawn the words cut through the air like a whip-lash. Every man in the company heard, and a dozen faces turned upwards.

'Well?' asked von Stalhein harshly.

'You can't do that.'

'Why not?'

'If you were the officer and gentleman I have hitherto supposed you to be, it would not be necessary for me to tell you,' answered Biggles coldly. 'It's murder; that's why.'

Von Stalhein moved slightly. 'I'm taking no more chances with you people,' he said bitterly. 'You'll share the same fate when you fall into my hands.'

'Never mind about us; I'm talking about that boy. I know what you're doing and I think I know who you are acting for. But whether you are acting for your government or whether you are simply out for personal gain, is of no importance. You cannot commit murder, for that is what the shooting of an unarmed man amounts to. We are not at war now, remember. If that boy has broken any of the laws of your country, send him up for trial; send us all up for trial. We'll stand or fall by a German jury; but your countrymen would never stand for what you're doing. We've fought in the past, you and I, but we fought fair. Even in that branch of service in which we were once engaged there were certain rules. Kill your man in a fight, yes, but even at war we did not murder unarmed men.'

A shot rang out as one of the green guards threw up his rifle. A piece of masonry flew from the wall not a foot from Biggles' head; a splinter struck him over the eye and a trickle of blood flowed down his cheek to his chin. But he did not move; he did not even flinch.

'Disarm that man, von Stalhein,' he said curtly. 'A

man so undisciplined as to fire without orders in the presence of his superior officer is a disgrace to his uniform and has no right to bear weapons. You were once a soldier; I should not like to think that you had become a common assassin.'

Even at that distance Algy saw the German's face flush scarlet. There was a sharp word of command, and the man who had fired grounded his weapon.

'Thank you,' acknowledged Biggles. 'And now, von Stalhein,' he continued, 'I have only one thing more to say. Go through with what you have started and I'll see to it that every newspaper in Europe prints the story on its front page of how Erich von Stalhein, once Captain in the Imperial Army blackened his hands with cold-blooded murder by shooting an unarmed man without trial. It will show the world how low Germany has fallen. Forbear, and I'll come down, unarmed, alone, to discuss the position as between gentlemen.'

Von Stalhein moved uncomfortably. 'Do you think you are in a position to dictate terms to me?' he inquired icily.

'Whether I am or not, I'm doing it,' returned Biggles. 'And it's time you knew me well enough to know that I'll do what I say. I'm not given to threatening; but go your own way and you sign your death-warrant. I'll see to that; I'll hunt you down and kill you like a mangy wolf, if I have to spend the rest of my life doing it.'

Von Stalhein hesitated. 'Very well,' he said at last, 'come down and we will talk the matter over.' There was another word of command. The firing-party sloped their rifles, lined up beside the prisoner, and disappeared through a small door in the wall. Von Stalhein turned on his heel, and without another upward glance, entered the castle.

Biggles drew back. His face was deathly pale and beads of perspiration stood out on his forehead. 'I pulled it off,' he said hoarsely, 'but I didn't think I should. It was touch and go. There is one way of dealing with a Prussian of the old military school like von Stalhein. See you later.'

'Where are you going?'

'Below, of course.'

'But what about me?'

'Stay where you are. You're not included in the deal, but I expect they'll come up for you. You'll have to act as you think best.'

'I see,' replied Algy slowly.

Biggles walked quickly to the trap-door, threw it open and climbed down into the attic. Then, without making any pretence of concealment, he walked quickly towards the staircase.

Before he reached it he met two of the green guards. They were evidently coming to meet him, for when they saw him they stopped and waited for him to come up to them; when he reached them they fell in in front and behind him, and with a curt gesture turned about and led the way to von Stalhein's study.

The German was seated in the same chair and in the same position as on the occasion of the fiasco with the musket the previous evening. For the moment he did not speak, but regarded Biggles with a most extra-ordinary expression in which wonder, hostility, and respect were mingled.

Biggles nodded affably. 'Well here we are again,' he observed. 'Quite like old times, eh?'

'A moment, please,' replied von Stalhein haughtily.

For a few seconds he looked at the people in front of him attentively, as if unable to make up his mind as to the best procedure. There was Biggles, quietly at ease regardless of the menacing rifles on either side of him; his guards, typical Prussians, bitterly hostile; another group of guards, with Ginger, dirty and dishevelled, amongst them. His eyes were no longer bandaged. Von Stalhein regarded them all in turn; then, as if his mind were made up, he spoke swiftly in German.

The senior guard saluted, barked an order, and watched his men file out of the door. Again he saluted—the queer, thrice-repeated German military salute, accompanied by a little bow—and withdrew.

Von Stalhein opened the middle drawer of his desk, took out a Mauser revolver and laid it down in front of him. 'Draw up a chair and sit down,' he said in an expressionless voice. 'Please be very careful. It is hardly necessary for me to say that I am in no mood to tolerate nonsense.'

Biggles fetched a leather-covered chair from a place near the desk and sat down. 'I can well believe it,' he said seriously. 'One way and another, I must be rather a nuisance.'

The German ignored the observation. 'Who is this?' he asked nodding towards Ginger.

'Merely a protégé of mine.'

'I see. Very well; tell him to sit down and keep still.'

Biggles complied, and Ginger took a seat nearer to the window.

'And where is Lacey?' asked von Stalhein.

'I left him on the roof, so I assume he is still there,' answered Biggles.

'My men will fetch him, no doubt,' returned the German. 'Now I do not propose to waste time in conventionalities,' he continued quickly. 'Do not misunderstand the position. At the slightest sign of trouble or resistance from you I shall shoot. My patience is at an end. My men are outside the door. One cry; one suspicious noise, and they will enter and fire without waiting for orders. Those are my instructions. And in case you wonder why I sent them out of the room, I will tell you. Some of them—I'm not sure which—speak a few words of English, and I would rather they did not hear what I have to say. Have I made myself clear?'

'Quite. May I trouble you for a cigarette?'

'Certainly.' Von Stalhein pushed his case and a box of matches across the desk. Then he fixed his cold blue eyes on Biggles' face. 'Will you tell me,' he said, helping himself to a cigarette, 'for whom you are working in this business?'

'I am working for a man named Cronfelt.'

The German suddenly grew tense. He remained rigid while the lighted match he was holding burnt down and scorched his finger. But he never took his eyes from Biggles' face. 'For whom did you say?' he asked in a curious voice.

'Cronfelt—or, to be more precise, a firm by the name of Cronfelt & Carstairs. You have heard of them, I see.'

'Yes,' answered the other slowly—very slowly. 'Are you serious? I mean, are you speaking the truth?'

Biggles frowned. 'I may lie when it is necessary, but at present it isn't,' he returned coldly.

A flicker of a smile crossed von Stalhein's face. 'Sorry,' he said. 'But how did it come about? That is, how did you come to meet Cronfelt?'

'He came to me one day when I was flying at Brooklands and asked me to operate an air-service for him. I did so, and I am still flying for him. But why ask me these questions? You know all this. You know as much as I do, or I've got my facts all wrong,' concluded Biggles.

Von Stalhein looked at him stonily. 'Perhaps,' he said with an odd smile. 'Perhaps.'

'Where you made the blunder, if I may say so,' went on Biggles, 'was in holding Lacey here. That was bound to bring me to the place sooner or later, even if your fellows hadn't brought me. So what has happened is entirely your fault.'

'Did Cronfelt personally give you the box, alleged to contain diamonds, to take to Amsterdam?' inquired von Stalhein, ignoring Biggles' frank comments.

'Of course.'

The German bit his lip thoughtfully. 'By the way,' he said raising his eyebrows, 'I hope Lacey still has those jewels of mine safely.'

'Jewels? What jewels?'

'You're not going to tell me you don't know what I mean?'

'I most certainly am.'

'Ridiculous.'

'Have it your own way.'

Von Stalhein looked puzzled. 'I suppose it is possible that in the excitement he forgot to tell you,' he said reflectively. 'You saw the jewels on my desk last night when you made your ill-timed entry?'

'I did.'

'After Lacey had knocked the lamp over he must have grabbed the jewels before he bolted. At least, that is what I assume, for they disappeared from that moment.'

'Then I hope you're right,' grinned Biggles. 'They'll probably come in handy.' He spoke naturally, but his finger-nails were digging into the palms of his hands, for while von Stalhein was speaking he had seen something that had set his nerves tingling so violently that he was afraid the German would notice the change in him. A small piece of solidified soot had fallen down the chimney into the great fireplace behind the man to whom he was speaking. Was it a fluke? A natural occurrence, or . . . He saw that von Stalhein was watching him closely.

'Well, I hope he still has them when he is taken—for all your sakes,' continued von Stalhein meaningly. 'I have been very worried about them, I must confess. In fact, they were the real reason for the little drama I staged this morning.'

It was Biggles' turn to start. 'Staged! How do you mean—staged?' he asked abruptly. He was genuinely astonished, but he did not fail to notice another particle of soot that fell into the hearth.

'You don't suppose I really intended shooting that boy, do you?' smiled the German.

The corners of Biggles' mouth turned down. 'You're bluffing,' he asserted belligerently.

'No I'm not—but I was. I knew you were about the building somewhere so I staged a little play, loudly, for your benefit, knowing that when you saw what was going on you would show up—as indeed you did.'

'Very clever,' admitted Biggles, moistening his lips and looking straight into the blue eyes opposite, for he dare not look at the fireplace in which a foot was now swinging, seeking a hold. 'But what's going to be the end of all this?' he went on quickly in a louder tone, for he was afraid that von Stalhein would hear what he could see.

'I'm coming to that in a minute,' replied von Stalhein, leaning forward on the desk. It was almost as if he sensed danger and wished to be nearer the revolver, yet was loth to admit his nervousness. 'There are one or two more questions I would like to ask first, though,' he added.

'Wait a minute; isn't this rather one-sided?' cried Biggles. 'What about letting me ask a few questions for a change?'

Von Stalhein frowned. 'You are here to answer questions, not to ask them,' he said harshly.

Only by sheer effort of will did Biggles overcome an almost overpowering desire to look at the fireplace, in which Algy, soot begrimed and unarmed, was now standing. He turned his head and looked at Ginger, and his admiration for his acting went up with a bound, for the lad was gazing disinterestedly towards the window, although he must have seen Algy. His attitude was one of bored nonchalance, although Biggles knew that every nerve in his body must be quivering with the excitement of the moment.

Von Stalhein went on speaking, and Biggles strove to listen, but the tension was terrible, and he felt that if Algy did not soon do something he would unconsciously make some move or sign that would betray him. He knew the reason for the delay. Algy was looking for a weapon, something within reach, but here was nothing. True, there were the fire-irons, but in keeping with the fire-place they were enormous, and to move them without making a noise was next to impossible.

Biggles became aware that von Stalhein was looking

at him oddly; his hand was creeping towards the revolver.

What would have happened during the next minute is impossible to say, but at that moment a motor-car horn of a peculiar note sounded outside, and an instant later wheels could be heard crunching on the gravel.

Von Stalhein rose to his feet, obviously agitated. 'I'm afraid we must postpone the rest of this interview until a more propitious occasion,' he said sharply. 'I have an important visitor.' He turned towards the door. His intention was plain. He was about to call the guards to take the prisoners into custody. But no sound came from his lips, for at that precise instant Algy sprang. He shot through the air like a cat, with arms outspread.

Von Stalhein heard him move, and half turned, but it was too late for him to do anything. Algy's left hand closed over his mouth and his right wrapped itself about his throat like the tentacle of an octopus.

Biggles was across the desk in a flash, snatching up the revolver by the muzzle as he went. It was no time to be squeamish. His arm flew up, and he brought the butt down sideways on the German's closely cropped head. He hated doing it, but it was a matter of life or death now, and he had no alternative.

Von Stalhein collapsed limply, and Algy staggered as he allowed the inert weight to slip to the floor.

Biggles thrust the revolver into his pocket and darted across the room to the door. The key was inside. He turned it as quietly as possible and then sped to the open window. Not a word was spoken. It was almost as though he were playing a well-rehearsed part.

Ginger had sprung to his feet and still stood by his chair, obviously at a loss to know what to do. Algy, breathing heavily, still stood over the unconscious

German. Through the soot on his face showed signs of the strain of the last few minutes.

Biggles was the first to speak. 'Come on,' he said quietly. 'This window is our only chance; the corridor is full of guards.'

The others joined him at the window and found themselves looking down over the main entrance to the castle, some twelve or fourteen feet below. At the foot of the steps that led to the door stood a dark-coloured limousine, evidently the vehicle that had brought the new-comer whose unexpected arrival had distracted von Stalhein, and who was now presumably inside the building. The chauffeur was a few yards away, examining a flower-bed with casual interest.

Biggles threw his legs over the sill. 'Make it snappy,' he said as he lowered himself to the full extent of his arms, and then released his hold.

The chauffeur heard the noise, as he was bound to, and hurried towards his charge, clearly not knowing quite what to make of things. But as Algy and Ginger followed their leader he realized that something was wrong and broke into a run, at the same time letting out a shout of warning.

Biggles whipped out the revolver. 'Back,' he snarled.

The German cowered. He may, or he may not, have understood the word, but the meaning of the blue muzzle of the revolver was unmistakable.

Biggles passed the revolver to Algy. 'Watch him,' he said tensely, and scrambled into the driver's seat. The others got in behind. For a few seconds Biggles juggled with the self-starter and the gears, and then the car shot forward.

The chauffeur let out a yell that was echoed inside the castle, but the car was moving swiftly now.

171

Biggles had no choice of roads: there was only one. He swung round the corner of the courtyard into which he had looked down a short time before, and the open road lay before him, sloping down steeply to a bend where it disappeared into the pinewood. There was no one in sight, and his foot depressed the accelerator with fierce exultation.

Ginger recovered his voice with a rush. 'Careful — the gates,' he yelled.

'Where?' shouted Biggles, startled, as he tore round the bend, and saw the gates in front of him — heavy wrought iron barriers which some green guards were feverishly closing. They were less than twenty yards away, and he could not have stopped even if he had wanted to. Collision was inevitable whatever he did. Instinctively he applied the brakes to lessen the shock of impact, but the car was still travelling at high speed when it struck.

Fortunately the gates were not fastened or the ride would have ended there and then. The men who were in the act of closing them instinctively leapt aside as the car bore down on them, leaving them slightly ajar, and watched the crash helplessly.

At the moment before the impact Biggles braced himself, and flung an arm over his face to ward off flying glass, and the others did the same. Actually, the big headlights which projected in front of the bonnet absorbed most of the shock, but even so the jar was sufficient to throw the three occupants forward. Biggles pitched over the wheel with a grunt but did not lose control. A cloud of steam spurted from the radiator. The gates flew wide open, struck the buffer-posts with a metallic clang, and then flew back again, just catching the rear mud-guards, but without impeding the progress of the car, which went on down the hill as if nothing had happened.

'Which way, Ginger?' called Biggles. 'Where did you leave the machine? We shan't get far in this car; the telephones are buzzing already, I'll be bound.'

'Straight ahead through the village,' answered Ginger, mopping his nose, which was bleeding, for he had bumped it violently on the seat in front of him. 'I couldn't find a landing-place within a couple of miles or so.'

They passed on through the village without interference, although they saw three or four of the green guards, and several curious glances were thrown at the car. In fact, it was a perfectly straightforward run, and five minutes saw them in a narrow lane under a hedge which Ginger declared concealed the machine.

The hedge may have hidden the Falcon from the road, but it did not prevent its discovery, as they soon ascertained when they pulled up and climbed over the field gate. The usual little crowd had collected, and although they regarded the airmen with surprise and some suspicion, no one made a move to prevent them from starting the propeller. Biggles automatically took the joystick, while the others filled the vacant seats. As he took off over the lane his wheels passed within a few feet of another car that was tearing along it at a dangerous speed, and he caught sight of a green uniform behind the wheel. He jabbed his thumb towards it. 'Too bad,' he shouted above the noise of the engine. 'They're just too late.'

But Algy was peering forward through the windscreen at the field in which he had left the 'Bulldog'. There was no sign of it. 'What about *my* machine,' he asked, anxiously.

173

Biggles shook his head. 'It looks as if we shall have to write it off as a dead loss,' he declared, 'unless you feel like going back for it,' he added, with a smile.

'No, I don't think it matters,' answered Algy quickly. 'I can buy another "Bulldog", but I can't buy another life.'

'That's what I was thinking,' Biggles told him lightly, as he settled down for the long flight home.

Chapter 12
Hardwick Again

I

It was about half-past nine the same morning when the Falcon landed at Hardwick airport after one stop at a small club aerodrome in northern France to refuel.

Biggles could see Smyth standing on the tarmac, staring upwards, before he landed, but by the time he was on the ground the mechanic had been joined by another man, immaculately dressed in morning clothes. There was no mistaking him. It was Cronfelt. This was something Biggles had not bargained for, and for a moment or two he was at a loss how to act, for he was unprepared for what he felt might be a difficult interview, and one that he would have preferred to postpone until he had decided on a course of action. But a meeting was now inevitable. Judging by his actions, Smyth had already identified the machine and would have told Cronfelt; and although the mechanic could not know who was in it, there was no way of avoiding the issue. So he taxied in, looking as unconcerned as possible.

Smyth ran out to guide the machine in, but when he saw who was at the joystick he staggered back and allowed the wing to pass him without making the slightest attempt to grab it. But he recovered quickly, and by the time Biggles had switched off and jumped to

175

the ground he had caught up with the machine. Algy and Ginger followed Biggles on to the tarmac.

Cronfelt moved forward to meet them. 'Ah! here you are; I've been waiting for you,' he said easily.

Biggles blinked and then looked away, as if the greeting struck him as being quite a natural one. Actually, it was far from that. Smyth, obviously, had seen a report of Biggles' death; his astonishment at seeing him was proof of that, for his behaviour had been in perfect accordance with his presumption. Cronfelt, on the other hand, expressed no such surprise, either by word or action. Yet it was preposterous to suppose that the head of the company had not heard of the crash at Aix. Even if he had not seen a report, Smyth would have told him about it. Why, then, did he express no surprise at seeing all three airmen? Biggles thought he knew. He looked back at his employer. 'Sorry I'm late,' he said, 'but we had rather a difficult run.'

'So I understand,' replied Cronfelt quickly. 'There is a report, you know, that you have been killed in a crash in France.'

'You didn't believe it, evidently.'

'No, of course not. I knew you'd get through all right. The others—Carstairs and his daughter and your mechanic—were very upset, but I tried to reassure them.'

'Nice of you to have so much confidence in me,' murmured Biggles slowly, although his brain was racing, wondering how much Cronfelt really knew, and how much he ought to tell him. It struck him as remarkable that so far his employer had not mentioned the object of his last trip or questioned him about the safety of the jewels. If he was not anxious about these

176

things why was he here on the tarmac? He was soon to know.

'I want you to run me over to Paris right away,' went on Cronfelt casually.

Biggles stared in unaffected amazement. 'To Paris?' he repeated. 'When?'

'Now—at once.'

Biggles recovered himself. 'I'm sorry, but that's quite impossible.' he said. 'The Cormorant—'

'This machine—the one you have just landed in—will do.'

'But it belongs to Miss Carstairs.'

'Oh, that's all right. She won't mind my using it,' answered Cronfelt easily. 'If you're tired, perhaps one of the others would fly me over,' he added.

'It isn't that. It will take a little time to get the machine ready.'

'Why?'

'Well, it's got to be refuelled, for one thing, and it ought to be looked over. An aeroplane should be examined every time it takes the air.'

'I'm prepared to take the risk.'

'You may be, but I'm not.'

'How long will it take to get ready?'

Biggles thought swiftly. 'I want a cup of tea and a wash.' he said. 'The others will attend to the machine. I'll tell you what I'll do. Give me three-quarters of an hour and I'll be ready to start. You needn't hang about here; go along to the refreshment buffet at the main entrance and have a drink while you're waiting.'

Cronfelt looked relieved. 'Very well,' he agreed. 'But don't be longer than you can help, will you? I'll go and fetch my suit-case.'

Biggles started. 'Where is it?' he asked.

'In your office.'

'You needn't drag that about with you; if you like I'll put it in the office safe.'

'That will do splendidly.'

Biggles led the way through to the office, opened the safe with his key, put the small suit-case inside, and locked it again. Then he threw off his jacket. 'See you in three-quarters of an hour,' he said pointedly.

'All right. It's now a quarter to ten; I'll be back at ten thirty.'

'O.K.'

With a curt nod Cronfelt departed. Biggles listened for a moment to the retreating footsteps, then crossed to the window, and saw his employer walking briskly down the tarmac towards the main entrance. He went to the door. 'Algy—Ginger—Smyth,' he called. 'Come here—jump to it . . . Now,' he went, when they were all assembled. 'I want you to do something. Listen carefully . . .'

II

At twenty-five minutes past ten Biggles put on his jacket, picked up his flying-cap and goggles, and walked towards the entrance to the hangar just as Cronfelt came bustling round the corner. His face was a trifle pale. 'Are you ready?' he asked in a slightly strained voice.

'Not quite; you're five minutes early.' Biggles nodded towards the Falcon, where Smyth and Ginger were standing by the propeller; Algy was in the cockpit. 'They're just starting up,' he said. 'We shall have to give her a couple of minutes to get warm.'

'I see.' Cronfelt moved closer, and his manner

became confidential. 'Listen, Bigglesworth,' he said. 'I want to have a few words with you in private.'

Biggles raised his eyebrows. 'Certainly,' he agreed. 'What about going through to the office? We've got to got and fetch your bag, anyway.'

'Excellent.'

'Well, what's the trouble?' inquired Biggles calmly as they entered the room.

'It's this. While I was over there in the main hall I saw a machine come in—one of the big liners—and I noticed the way the passengers were dealt with at the customs barrier. Tell me, are they just as strict at the Paris aerodrome—what do you call the place?

'Bourget. Yes, they're pretty thorough.'

'I had no idea there were all these formalities. I thought—'

'You could just land and stroll away?'

'No, not exactly that, but—'

'Why beat about the bush? You don't want to go through customs, is that it?'

'Well—er—I—that is—'

'Oh, come on, man; what *do* you mean?'

'Yes, I suppose you're right. To tell the truth, I have accidentally allowed my passport to lapse—only noticed it this morning. Couldn't you land me somewhere else? I mean, an aeroplane isn't like a ship, which puts you ashore at a special place. You can land anywhere, and no one would be the wiser.'

'Don't kid yourself, Mr Cronfelt. If it was as easy as that aeroplanes would do a roaring trade, and no one would pay duty on anything. But you want to land at an unauthorized place—is that it?'

'Yes.'

'Then I'm afraid there's nothing doing. I'm not prepared to risk losing my licence.'

Cronfelt mopped his face with his handkerchief. 'I'd make it worth your while,' he said in a low voice. 'Would a hundred pounds — cash — be an inducement?'

Biggles glanced out of the window. Subconsciously he saw a low-wing monoplane, bearing German registration letters, make a neat landing. 'No,' he said slowly, 'I'm afraid it wouldn't. My price, when I break the law, will be more than you will be prepared to pay.'

Cronfelt's jaw set at an ugly angle. 'Very well,' he said harshly. 'Give me my bag; I'll find some one who'll be more accommodating.'

Biggles unlocked the safe and put the suit-case on the table. Cronfelt reached for it, but Biggles kept his hand on it.

'Just a moment, Mr. Cronfelt,' he said coolly. 'As a reserve officer of the Royal Air Force, I am within my rights in demanding to know just what you have in this bag that makes you so anxious to evade customs.'

Cronfelt stiffened, and looked at Biggles with blazing eyes. His right hand went into his pocket. 'So,' he sneered, 'you feel like that. Then you should have procured assistance before you tackled a job of this sort.'

'As a matter of fact I did,' replied Biggles easily with a faint smile. Then raising his voice, 'Colonel Raymond,' he called.

The door of the adjacent room, which was Biggles' sleeping apartment, was pushed open and four men moved in swiftly. The first was Colonel Raymond. The second was Sir Guy Brunswick. The other two men were strangers to Biggles, but they were obviously what is known in police circles as 'plain-clothes men'.

Cronfelt knew it, too, and acted with a speed that

Biggles did not believe possible. He whipped out an automatic and fired point-blank at his accuser. But Biggles leapt aside, and one of the plain-clothes men swung round as the bullet took him in the shoulder.

Before any of them had recovered from the shock, for the swift, desperate move had taken everybody by surprise, Cronfelt had snatched up the bag and disappeared through the door. Biggles flung himself at it, but the key grated on the other side. 'The window,' he shouted, and made a dash for the only other exit. By the time he was through Cronfelt was racing down the tarmac towards his car.

'By heavens, he'll do it,' cried Raymond over Biggles' shoulder.

But he was mistaken, for the drama took an utterly unexpected turn, and what followed left the spectators almost stunned by its very suddenness.

Walking up the edge of the tarmac, along the line where it met the turf, was a tall, slim man in flying overalls. He was looking about him as a man who is in a strange place, but is seeking a definite object. A short distance behind him a low-wing monoplane was being taxied over the smooth grass. There was nothing unusual about this. Indeed, the sight was so commonplace that not one of the men who poured through the office window paid the slightest attention to either the man or the machine, even if they noticed them

Cronfelt, in making for his car, had to pass within a few yards of the stranger, and it is doubtful if he noticed him either—that is, not until he spoke. What he said no one but Cronfelt could hear, but the words were sufficient to cause the running man to swerve in his stride.

There was a flash and a report. Cronfelt staggered;

the suit-case flew out of his hand, and he pitched forward on to his face and lay twitching convulsively. A little cloud of pale blue smoke floated away from the stranger's hand. Unhurriedly he stepped closer to the man on the ground and fired five more shots into him at point-blank range. Then he picked up the suitcase, glanced at the little crowd racing towards him, turned on his heel, and walked calmly across to the monoplane. Somebody inside pushed open the cabin door, and he stepped in. The engine roared, and the machine swept over the turf into the air.

Biggles stopped and passed his hand wearily over his face. 'Did you ever see anything so cool as that in your life?' he gasped.

Colonel Raymond also stopped. 'Ring for the ambulance,' he said crisply to the plain-clothes man who had accompanied him. 'Better tell them to send a doctor—not that he'll be able to do much good. The first shot was enough, judging by the way Cronfelt fell.' He turned to Biggles. 'Do you want to go on—'

Biggles grimaced. 'Not me,' he said.

'Good, then let's go back. There are a lot of things I want to ask you. Pity the fellow got away with the suit-case; there must have been something very valuable in it.'

A flicker of a smile crossed Biggles' face. 'There was,' he said quietly.

Chapter 13
Biggles Tells The Story

They all walked back to the hangar, and were just going through to the office when a small car pulled up with a jerk and Carstairs jumped out. 'All right, Stella; leave the car where it is,' he told his daughter, who was at the wheel. Then, turning to the others, 'Where's Cronfelt?' he snapped. He took a pace backward as he caught sight of Biggles. 'You!' he gasped. 'But they said you had been killed.'

'Who said? inquired Biggles.

'Everybody—Cronfelt—the newspapers!'

'Well, as you see, they were all wrong,' smiled Biggles. 'Good-morning, Miss Carstairs,' he went on. 'Don't look so pained, or I shall feel I have made a mistake in coming back to life.'

Stella did not reply. She merely stared unbelievingly.

'But where's Cronfelt?' cried Carstairs again, looking round.

'He's on his way to the mortuary, I expect,' Biggles told him.

'Good heavens! Has somebody been killed?'

'Yes.'

'Who?'

'He has.'

'*Who?*'

'Cronfelt.'

'Cronfelt—killed? How did it happen?'

'He got in the way of a bullet travelling in the opposite direction.'

Carstairs sat down suddenly on an empty oil drum.

'You're not going to shed tears about it, I hope?'

'I am not,' burst out the old man. 'The man was a thief.'

'You were a long time finding that out.'

'He has bolted with all our available funds. Did he have a suit-case with him?'

'He did.'

'Where is it?'

'In an aeroplane—on its way to Germany, I expect. The man who shot him collared it.'

Carstairs appeared to age ten years in a minute of time. 'Then I am ruined,' he said resignedly.

'Let's go through into the office and I'll tell you what I know about the affair,' suggested Biggles.

'Yes, I think it's time we had the facts,' put in Colonel Raymond quietly.

They all went through into the office and sat down on anything available. Biggles pulled out the desk chair for Stella. Sir Guy and Colonel Raymond sat on the table. Algy squatted on a box and Ginger leaned against the door.

'Now,' said Colonel Raymond tersely, 'go ahead.'

'Just a minute,' replied Biggles, crossing over to the safe. He unlocked it and pulled out a filing-basket, which he placed on the table. 'Does anybody want any money?' he grinned, stacking up piles of bank and treasury notes beside the basket.

For a moment nobody spoke.

'Speak up,' he insisted.

'Where did all this come from?' asked Raymond in a high-pitched voice.

'This is what Cronfelt was getting away with. I took the precaution of emptying his suit-case while he was away waiting for us to get the machine ready, and made up the weight with some books which I hope my friend von Stalhein will appreciate when he finds them.'

Sir Guy Brunswick was staring at the notes. 'This is a very serious business,' he said.

Biggles glanced up. 'You'd have thought so if you'd been with us last night,' he said grimly. 'Ah, this is what I was looking for.' He took out a morocco leather case, flicked it open, and gazed at the contents admiringly. 'Aren't they just too sweet?' he murmured.

Carstairs let out an exclamation of delight. 'Thank heavens!' he cried. 'They're the diamonds that should have gone to Amsterdam. I thought we'd lost them.'

'I expect the money is yours, too.' Biggles pushed the piles of notes towards Carstairs. 'Take it.' he said. 'And if you have got any sense you'll give it to your daughter to take care of. She's better qualified for the job than you are, if I may say so. There's just one other thing.' Biggles felt in his pocket and produced the case of jewels that Algy had taken from von Stalhein's desk the previous evening. 'Anybody know anything about these?' he inquired.

Sir Guy took a quick pace forward. 'Great goodness! they're the Devereux diamonds,' he said tersely. 'They were stolen in transit between Paris and London some time ago. My firm paid a hundred thousand pounds insurance on them. How on earth did you get hold of them?'

'Oh, we just picked them up in our travels yesterday—at least, Algy here did. Thank him, not me.'

'And now, if you've finished your conjuring tricks, what about this report?' protested Colonel Raymond.

'This is an important affair, and I must get back to the Yard.'

Biggles walked over and leaned against the window through which he had made such a hasty exit a short time ago. 'I'll let you have a written report in due course,' he said. 'I haven't time to tell you everything now because it would take too long, but I can just run over the main points.'

'Do, by all means,' agreed the Assistant Commissioner.

Biggles tapped a cigarette reflectively on his case. 'You all remember the beginning of this affair, so I needn't go over it all again,' he began. 'Cronfelt came to me and asked me to run an airline for him. The same evening some one rang me up on the telephone from Germany and told me not to accept the proposition. Those two facts at once provided me with a fairly substantial background upon which to work. Remember, Cronfelt had not come to me entirely under his own steam, so to speak. He had never heard of me. He came to me because my name was suggested to him by you, Raymond, the reason being that you were as interested as anybody in clearing up this affair. In the circumstances he could hardly refuse to act on your suggestion; further, his astute mind had already seen possibilities of profiting to a far greater extent than by merely following the instructions of the people for whom he was working. For Cronfelt was by no means his own boss.

'We didn't know that at the time, of course, but as I see it now, the position was this. His principals, whom I shall be able to tell you something about later on, wanted gold. Whether they were working for themselves, or for some big syndicate, or for some national organization, I still do not know for certain, but I suspect the last. We all know there is no gold in Germany, and certain interests there must be finding it difficult to get along without it. How could they get some? By one way only, which was helping themselves to the metal that was being rushed constantly between London and Paris by bullion dealers and banks to balance currency fluctuations. There is no doubt in my mind that the job for which Cronfelt was detailed was to put himself in a position from which he could advise his principals of such gold movements, leaving them to do the rest. And for a time he succeeded. Then, what with the public complaining, and the insurance people getting suspicious, things became more difficult.

'But when things began to buzz he got another idea. If he could insure the gold he would score two ways. He would have his share of the stolen gold, or its value, and he would also have the insurance money. Very nice. Gems could be handled in the same way. A German airline was started, but the people over this side smelt a rat, and that was that. Now let us see what happened when I stepped on to the stage.

'Cronfelt rang up his head lad and told him he was starting a British airline, which ought to make it easier to get hold of the gold. All so well and good. But when he mentioned my name as pilot, it didn't sound so good to the man at the other end of the wire. Because that man knew me. His name is Erich von Stalhein. You remember him, Raymond? For the benefit of the others, I may say that von Stalhein was on the German Intelligence Staff during the war at the time I was working for British Intelligence, and we got tangled up. And make no mistake: the people who put von Stalhein on to this latest job knew what they were doing, for he is a bright lad. But let us go on.

'I can well imagine that when von Stalhein learnt that I was to be the pilot he got a bit worried, and he probably told Cronfelt to find another man. But that was going to be difficult. You, Raymond, might have asked why, and failing a very good reason, might have become suspicious. Cronfelt may have told von Stalhein that, so von Stalhein tried another dodge. He rang me up and tried to warn me off. I knew the voice but I couldn't place him because I thought he'd been killed. But that is another story. Instead of taking the warning, I hooked up to Cronfelt & Carstairs, as you know.

'Things soon started to go wrong for the opposition, and I don't take any great credit for that, because from the very beginning it was clear that some one in a well-informed position was keeping the enemy posted, both in the matter of gold shipments and internal arrangements. I got my first straight clue that Cronfelt was the man when he told me after I had run the first lot of gold through that the manager of the Bank of France had told him that a robbery had taken place. I pressed the questions deliberately because the manager had told me that he had not told any one. After I left Cronfelt I rang up the manager and asked him if he had told Cronfelt. He said "No." Therefore Cronfelt was lying. Why? We know now that the probability is that the crooks had rung up and told him either what had happened or what they expected to happen, and he had to account for the fact that he knew. So he thought he was quite safe in saying that the manager had told him. But it was clear to me that he had *anticipated* the robbery, to say the least of it. Further, he seemed rather upset when I told him that I had fixed an explosive charge in each of the dummy bullion boxes—which was purely an imaginative effort on my part. Why should he be upset? He didn't strike me as the sort of fellow who would be squeamish. No, it began to look as if friend Cronfelt was playing an underhand game, and I set my clock accordingly, afterwards acting on the assumption that he would advise his head-quarters of everything that took place. And I was right. For instance, I told him about the false bottom in our machine, assuming that he would tell the gang. He did. Anyway, somebody told them, but as I had prepared things accordingly we got away with it again.

'He must have known that Algy had been taken prisoner. None of you except Miss Carstairs knew that, but he was. Cronfelt knew it—at least, I acted on the assumption that he would be told—and the situation presented an opportunity for him to feather his nest very handsomely. I expect his people were getting fed up with him, and he was looking for a chance to bring off a coup before packing up. As things transpired, his greed was his undoing. He was to send me to Amster-dam with a parcel of diamonds, knowing that I should use—or pretend to use—that same parcel to ransom Algy. He probably imagined that I was to be bumped off by the people who met me; but whether I was or not, only an empty package would be found in my possession. It was clever in its simplicity. his friends would assume that I had hidden the real package and made up a dummy. What could they do about it? Nothing! Meanwhile, Cronfelt had got the diamonds in his pocket.

'You see, if the crooks got in touch with Cronfelt and asked questions, he would be quite safe in saying that he had handed the diamonds to me as arranged. That would not have provided his headquarters with sufficient grounds for suspecting him of playing double, because it was quite on the boards that I *should* make up a dummy rather than allow the stones to fall into the hands of the enemy.

'But his plans came all unstuck, and the most tragic thing of all for him was when I came face to face with von Stalhein last night. He took my word for it that the parcel he had taken from me was the same one that Cronfelt had handed to me. It was empty. In any case, my astonishment at seeing the empty box was too real to be faked. I was as surprised as von Stalhein was. And he knew it.

'From that moment Cronfelt's number was up. Von Stalhein knew that he was playing his own hand and not working for the gang. I don't suppose we shall ever know the truth of what happened next. Whether von Stalhein rang him up, recalling him to Germany, and so making it clear that he was rumbled, or whether some friend at headquarters rang him up on the quiet — which is not unlikely — and told him that the game was up, we do not know; but whichever it was, Cronfelt decided that it was high time to go into retirement, for the arm of vengeance of his associates was likely to be a long one.

'I came back here this morning prepared to go to Scotland Yard and put all the facts I had gathered into your hands, Raymond. I had, in fact, left a letter behind me which you would have found interesting, but that doesn't matter now. But I got all hot and bothered when I landed here to find that Cronfelt was already on the tarmac waiting to be taken to Paris. I suppose I should have thought of that possibility, but I hadn't. I do not think for a moment that he had the remotest idea that I suspected him of being a crook—that is, not until I showed my hand in this room. It was rather odd. He probably knew that I had been to his head-quarters as a prisoner; that we had all been prisoners; he probably knew that we had escaped. Either way, whether he knew it or not, he expected to find us here— as indeed he did. He didn't want to talk about the diamonds or anything else. That was all over. He was concerned with one thing and that was getting out of the country as quickly as he could.

'Of the rest, you know as much as I do. Von Stalhein came over here to find Cronfelt—for I have no doubt who the man was who did the shooting. He wanted Cronfelt and he wanted the jewels. As soon as he knew that we had escaped he must have jumped straight into another machine and followed us over. He went to the telephone booth in the main hall and rang up the office to ask if Cronfelt was there, never suspecting that his man was actually on the aerodrome.'

'How did you know that?' asked the Colonel sharply.

'Because while he was away the London office rang up to confirm that Cronfelt was here, saying that a friend of his—friend, eh?—wanted to see him urgently, and they had told him that he was here. I attached no importance to it at the time, but it is plain enough now to see who the friend was.

'You see, when I found him here I hadn't much time to lose. I had to delay his departure. That was easy. I told him that the machine required attention, and sent him to the buffet to wait. As soon as he was out of the way, I rang you up, Raymond, and told you to come down here as quickly as possible. Then I emptied his suit-case, as you have seen, in case of accidents. And it was a good thing I did. I was surprised to find all that money, but I expected to find the jewels.

'Then came the show-down. Cronfelt bolted and ran into the very man from whom he was running away. Von Stalhein was no doubt looking for Biggles & Co.'s hangar at the time, and he was probably just as much surprised to see his man sprinting down the tarmac as Cronfelt was to see *him*. Well, Cronfelt got his deserts, and von Stalhein got the useless suit-case; which is all as it should be.'

'And that's all, eh?' inquired Sir Guy.

Biggles smiled. 'Nearly, but not quite,' he said softly. 'There is a little matter of a cheque for fifteen thousand pounds which you promised—'

'Ah! I thought perhaps you'd forgotten that,' smiled the baronet as he reached for his cheque-book.

Biggles shook his head sorrowfully. 'We may be airmen, but that doesn't mean we can live on air,' he said softly. 'Do you mind making the cheque out to Biggles & Co?'